SINKING INTO TROUBLE

Worsaw shot the private three times in the face. The body crumpled backward against—and partly through—the wall.

"That takes care of *one* son-of-a-bitch," said the spectral Worsaw.

Before the man's murderous inference could be realized, Hansard acted. In a single motion he threw himself from the bench and the attaché case that he had been holding at Worsaw's gun hand. The gun went off, doing harm only to the case.

In leaping from the bench Hansard had landed on the floor of the steel vault—or more precisely, in it, for his hands had sunk several inches into the steel, which felt like chilled turpentine against his skin. This was strange, really very strange . . . But not to be distracted from his immediate purpose—which was to disarm Worsaw—he sprang up to catch hold of Worsaw's hand, but found that with the same movement his legs sank knee-deep into the insubstantial floor.

echo round his bones

Thomas M. Disch

A BERKLEY MEDALLION BOOK
published by
BERKLEY PUBLISHING CORPORATION

BERKLEY MEDALLION EDITION, JANUARY, 1967

*BERKLEY MEDALLION BOOKS are published by
Berkley Publishing Corporation
15 East 26th Street, New York, N. Y. 10010*

Berkley Medallion Books ® TM 757,375

Printed in the United States of America

ECHO ROUND HIS BONES

ONE

NATHAN HANSARD

The finger on the trigger grew tense. The safety was released, and in almost the same moment the gray morning stillness was shattered by the report of the rifle. Then, just as a mirror slivers and the images multiply, a myriad echoes returned from the ripening April hillsides—a mirthful, mocking sound. The echoes re-echoed, faded, and died. But the stillness did not settle back on the land; the stillness was broken.

The officer who had been marching at the head of the brief column of men—a captain, no more—came striding back along the dirt track. He was a man of thirty-five or perhaps forty years, with fair, regular features now set in an expression of anger—or, if not quite anger, irritation. Some would have judged him a handsome man; others might have objected that his manner was rather too neutral—a neutrality expressive not so much of tranquility as of truce. His jaw was set and his lips molded in the military cast. His blue eyes were glazed by that years-long unrelenting discipline. They might not, it could be argued, have been by nature such severe features: without that discipline the jaw might have been more relaxed, the lips fuller, the eyes brighter—yes, and the captain might have been another man.

He stopped at the end of the column and addressed himself to the red-haired soldier standing on the outside of the last file—a master-sergeant, as might be ascertained from the chevron sewn to the sleeve of his fatigue jacket.

"Worsaw?"

"Sir." The sergeant came, approximately, to attention.

"You were instructed to collect all ammunition after rifle practice."

"Yes, sir."

"All cartridges were to be given back to you, therefore no one should have any ammunition now."

"No, sir."

"And this was done?"

"Yes, sir. So far as I know."

"And yet the shot we just heard was certainly fired by one of us. Give me your rifle, Worsaw."

With visible reluctance the sergeant handed his rifle to the captain. "The barrel is warm," the captain observed. Worsaw made no reply.

"May I take your word, Worsaw, that this rifle is unloaded?"

"Yes, sir."

The captain put the butt of the rifle against his shoulder and laid his finger over the trigger. He remarked that the safety was off. Worsaw said nothing.

"May I pull the trigger, Worsaw?" The rifle was pointed at the sergeant's right shin. Worsaw still said nothing, but beads of sweat had broken out on his freckled face.

"Do I have your permission? Answer me."

Worsaw broke down. "No, sir," he said.

The captain broke open the magazine and removed the cartridge clip. He handed the rifle back to the sergeant. "Is it possible, Worsaw, that the shot that brought us to a halt a moment ago was fired from this rifle?" There was, even now, no trace of sarcasm in the captain's voice.

"I saw a rabbit, sir—"

The captain's brow furrowed. "Did you hit it, Worsaw?"

"No, sir."

"Fortunately for you. Do you realize that it is a federal offense to kill wildlife on this land?"

"It was just a rabbit, sir. We shoot them around here all the time. Usually when we come out for rifle practice, or that sort of stuff—"

"Do you mean to say that it is *not* against the law?"

"No, sir, I wouldn't know about that. I just know that usually—"

"Shut up, Worsaw!"

Worsaw's face had become so red that his reddish-blond eyebrows and lashes seemed pale in comparison. In his bafflement his lower lip had begun to tic back and forth, as though some buried fragment of his character were trying to pout.

"I despise a liar," the captain said blandly. He inserted his thumbnail under the tip of the chevron sewn on Worsaw's right sleeve and ripped it off with one quick motion. Then the other chevron.

The captain returned to the front of the column, and the march back to the trucks that would return them to Camp Jackson was resumed.

This captain, who will be the hero of our history, was a man of the future—that is to say, of what would seem futurity to us; for to the captain it seemed the most commonplace present. Yet there are degrees of living in the future, of being contemporary there, and it must be admitted that in many ways the captain was more a man of the past (of his past, and even perhaps of ours) than of the future.

Consider only his occupation: A career officer in the Regular Army—surely a most uncharacteristic employment in the year 1990. By that time everyone knew that the army, the Regular Army (for though the draft was still in operation and young men were compelled to surrender their three years to the Reserve Army, they all knew that this was a joke; that the Reserves were useless; that they were maintained only as a device for keeping themselves out of the labor force, or off the unemployment rolls that much longer after college), was a career for louts and nincompoops. But if *everyone* knew this . . . ? Everyone who was "with it"; everyone who was truly comfortable living in the future.

These contemporaries of the captain (many of whom —some 29 per cent—were so much unlike him as to prefer three years of postgraduate study in the comfortable and permissive prisons that had been built for C.O.'s—the conchies, as they were called—rather than submit to the ritual nonactivities of the Reserves) regarded the captain and his like as—and this is their most charitable judgment—fossils.

It is true that military service traditionally requires qualities more of character than of intelligence. Does this mean, then, that our hero is on the stupid side? By no means! And to dispel any lingering doubts of this, let us hasten to note that in third grade the captain's I.Q., as measured by the Stanford-Binet Short Form, was a respectable 128—certainly as much or more than we can fairly demand of a hero in this line of work.

In fact it had been the captain's experience that he possessed intelligence in excess of his needs; he would often have been happier in his calling if he had been as blind to certain distinctions—often of a moral character —as most of his fellow officers seemed to be. Once, indeed, this over-acuteness had directly injured the captain's prospects. And it might be that that long-ago event was the cause, even this much later, of the captain's relatively low position (considering his age) in the military hierarchy. We shall have opportunity to hear more of this unpleasant moment—but in its proper place.

It may just as plausibly be the case that the captain's lack of advancement was due simply to a lack of vacancies. The Regular Army of 1990 was much smaller than the Army of our own time—partly because of international agreements, but basically in recognition of the fact that a force of 25,000 men was more than ample to prosecute a nuclear war—and this, in 1990, was the only war that the two great power blocs were equipped to fight.

Disarmament was a *fait accompli;* though it was of a kind that no one of our time had quite anticipated; instead of eliminating nuclear devices, it had preserved them alone. In truth, "disarmament" is something of a euphemism; what was done had been done more in the interests of domestic economy than of world peace. The bombs that the Pacifists complained of (and in 1990 *everyone*

10

was a Pacifist) were still up there, biding their time, waiting for the day that everyone agreed was inevitable. Everyone, that is, who was with it; everyone who was truly comfortable living in the future.

Thus, though the captain lived in the future he was very little representative of it. His political opinions were conservative to a point just short of reaction. He read few of what we would think of as the better books of his time; saw few of the better movies—not because he lacked aesthetic sensibilities—for instance, his musical taste was highly developed—but because these things were made for other, and possibly better, tastes than his.

He had no sense of fashion—and this was not a small lack, for among his contemporaries fashion was a potent force. Other-directedness had carried all before it; shame, not guilt, was the greater shaper of souls, and the most important question one could ask oneself was: *"Am I with it?"* And the captain would have had to answer, *"No."*

He wore the wrong clothes, in the wrong colors, to the wrong places. His hair was too short, though by present standards it would have seemed rather full for a military man; his face was too pale—he wouldn't use even the most discreet cosmetics; his hands were bare of rings. Once, it is true, there had been a gold band on the third finger of his left hand, but that had been some years ago.

Unfashionableness has its price, and for the captain the price had been steep. It had cost him his wife and son. She had been too contemporary for him—or he too outmoded for her. In effect their love had spanned a century, and though at first it was quite strong enough to stand the strain, in time it was the times that won. They were divorced on grounds of incompatibility.

At this point it may have occurred to the reader to wonder why in a tale of the future we should have chosen a hero so little representative of his age. It is an easy paradox to resolve, for the captain's position in the military establishment had brought him—or, more precisely, was soon to bring him—into contact with that

11

phenomenon which, of all the phenomena of his age, was most advanced, most contemporary, most at the forefront of the future—with, in short, the matter transmitter —or, in the popular phrase, the manmitter—or, in the still more popular phrase, the Steel Womb.

"Brought into contact" is perhaps too weak and passive a phrase. The captain's role was to be more heroic than such words would suggest. "Came into conflict" would do much better. Indeed he was to come into conflict with much more than the Steel Womb—with the military establishment as well, with society in general, and with himself. It could even be said, without stretching the meaning too far, that in his conflict he pitted himself against the nature of reality itself.

One final paradox before we re-embark upon this tale: It was to be this captain, the military man, the man of war, who was, at the last minute and by the most remarkable device, to rescue the world from that ultimate catastrophe—the war to end wars, the Armageddon that we are all, even now, waiting for. But by that time he would not be the same man, but a different man; a man quite thoroughly of the future—because he had made it in his own image.

At twilight of that same day on which we last saw him, the captain was sitting alone in the office of "A" Artillery Company. It was as bare a room as it could possibly be and yet be characterized as an office. On the gray metal desk were only an appointment calendar that showed the date to be the twentieth of April; a telephone, and a file folder containing brief statistical profiles of the twenty-five men under the captain's command: Barnstock, Blake, Cavender, Dahlgren, Doggett. . . .

The walls of the room were bare, except for framed photos, cut out of magazines, of General Samuel ("Wolf") Smith, Army Chief of Staff, and of President Lind, whose presence here would have to be considered as merely commemorative, since he had been assassinated some forty days before. As yet, apparently, no one had found a good likeness of Lee Madigan, his successor, to replace Lind's

12

photo. On the cover of *Life,* Madigan had been squinting into the sun; on *Time*'s cover he was shown splattered with the President's blood.

There was a metal file, and it was empty; a metal wastebasket, it was empty; metal chairs, empty. The captain cannot be held strictly to account for the bareness of the room, for he had been in occupancy only two days. Even so, it was not much different from the office he had left behind in the Pentagon Building, where he had been the aide of General Pittmann.

. . . Fanning, Green, Horner, Lesh, Maggit, Norris, Nelsen, Nelson. . . . They were Southerners mostly, the men of "A" Company; sixty-eight per cent of the Regular Army was recruited in Southern states, from the backwoods and back alleys of that country-within-a-country, the fossil society that produced fossil men. . . . Lathrop, Perigrine, Pearsall, Pearsall, Rand, Ross. . . . Good men in their way—that cannot be denied. But they were not, any more than their captain, contemporary with their own times. Plain, simple, honest men—Squires, Sumner, Truemile, Thorn, Worsaw, Young—but also mean-spirited, resentful, stupid men, as the captain well knew. You cannot justly expect anything else of men who have been outmoded; who have had no better prospect than *this*; who will never make much money, or have much fun or taste the sparkling elixir of being "With It," who are and always will be deprived—and who know it.

These were not precisely the terms with which the captain regarded this problem, though he had been long enough in the Army (since 1976) to realize that they did not misrepresent the state of affairs. But he looked at things on a reduced scale (he was only a captain, after all) and considered how to deal with the twenty-five men under his command so as to divert the full force of their resentment from his own person. He had expected to be resented; this is the fate of all officers who inherit the command of an established company. But he hadn't expected matters to go to such mutinous extremes as they had this morning after rifle drill.

Rifle drill was a charade. Nobody expected rifles to be

13

used in the next war. In much the same way, the captain suspected, this contest of wills between himself and his men was a charade—a form that had to be gone through before a state of equilibrium could be reached; a tradition-sanctioned period of mutual testing out. The captain's object was to abbreviate this period as much as possible; the company's to draw it out to their advantage.

The phone rang, the captain answered it. The orderly of Colonel Ives hoped that the captain would be free to see the colonel. Certainly, whenever it was convenient to the colonel. In half an hour? In half an hour. Splendid. In the meantime, perhaps, it would be possible for the captain to instruct "A" Company to prepare for a jump in the morning?

The captain felt his mouth grow dry; his blood quickened perceptibly. He was hardly aware of answering or of hanging up the receiver.

Prepare to jump. . . .

He seemed for a moment to fission, to become two men —an old man and a young man; and while the old man sat behind the bare desk, the young one stood crouched before the open hatch of an airplane, machine gun in hand (they *had* used small arms in that war), staring out into the vast brightness and down, far down, at the unfamiliar land, the improbable rice paddies. The land had been so *green*. And then he had jumped, and the land had come rushing up toward him. The land, in that instant, became his enemy, and he . . . Did he become the enemy of that land?

But the captain knew better than to ask himself such questions. A policy of deliberate and selective amnesia was the wisest. It had served him in good stead these twelve years.

He put on his hat, and went out through the door of the orderly room into a yard of unvigorous grass. Worsaw was sitting on the steps of the brick barracks building, smoking. The captain addressed him without thinking:

"Sergeant!"

Worsaw rose and stood to attention smartly. "Sir!"

"That is to say—" (Trying to make the blunder seem

14

a deliberate cruelty, and not—which was inadmissible—an error.) "—*Private* Worsaw. Inform the men that they are to be prepared to make a jump in the morning at eight hundred hours."

How quickly the clouds of resentment could overcast the man's pale eyes. But in an even tone Worsaw replied, "Yes, sir."

"And shine those shoes, Private. They're a disgrace to this company."

"Yes, *sir.*"

"You're in the Army now, Private. Don't you forget it."

"No, *sir.*"

As though, the captain thought wryly as he walked away, *he had any choice. Poor devil. As though he could forget it. As though any of us could.*

"This will be your first jump, won't it, Captain?"

"Yes, sir."

Colonel Ives laid a forefinger on the soft folds of his chin. "Let me caution you against expecting much, then. It will be no different there than it is here at Camp Jackson. You breathe the same air, see the same dome overhead, drink the same water, live in the same buildings, with the same men."

"Yes—so I've been told. But even so, it's hard to believe."

"There are *some* differences. For instance, you can't drive in to D.C. on the week ends. And there are fewer officers. It can become very boring."

"You wouldn't be able to tell me, I suppose, to whom I'll be reporting?"

Colonel Ives shook his head aggrievedly. "I don't know myself. Security around the Womb is absolute. It would be easier to break into heaven, or into Fort Knox. You'll receive your final instructions tomorrow, just before you go into the Womb, but not from me. I only work here."

Then why, the captain wondered, *did you have me come to see you?*

The colonel was not long in answering the unasked

question: "I heard about the little to-do you had this morning with the men."

"Yes—with Sergeant Worsaw."

"Ah—then you mean to say his rank has been restored already?"

"No. I'm afraid I was only speaking loosely."

"A shame that it had to happen. Worsaw is a good man, an absolutely topnotch technician. The men respect him —even the, um, colored boys. You're not a Southerner yourself, are you, Captain?"

"No, sir."

"Didn't think so. We Southerners are sometimes hard to explain to other folks. Take Worsaw now—a good man, but he does have a stubborn streak, and when he takes a notion into his head—" Colonel Ives clucked with dismay. "But a good man—we can't let ourselves forget that."

Colonel Ives waited until the captain had agreed to this last statement.

"Of course these things will happen. They're inevitable when you're taking over a new command. I remember, in my own case—did I tell you that I was once at the head of "A" Company myself? Yes, indeed! I had a little trouble with that fellow too. But I smoothed it over, and soon we were all working together like clockwork. Of course it was easier for me than it will be for you. I hadn't gone so far as to strip him of rank. That was a very strong gesture, Captain. I imagine you must have regretted it since?"

"No, sir. I was convinced at the time, and still am, that he merited it—amply."

"Of course, of course. But we must remember the Golden Rule, eh? 'Live and let live.' The Army is a team, and we've all got to pull together. You can't do your work without Worsaw, Captain, and I can't do my work without you. We can't let *prejudice*—" Colonel Ives paused to smile, "—or *temper* affect our judgment. Mutual co-opera-tion: that's the Army way. You co-operate with Worsaw, I co-operate with you."

The captain's attitude throughout this speech had been one of almost Egyptian stiffness. Now there was a long silence while Colonel Ives waited, bobbing his head up and down into his chins, for the captain to agree with him.

"Is that all, sir?" the captain asked.

"Now isn't that just like a Northerner? Always in a rush to be off somewhere else. Well, don't let *me* slow you down, Captain. But if I might offer a word of advice—though it's none of my business—"

"By all means, Colonel."

"I'd restore Worsaw's rank by the end of the week. I'm sure that will have been punishment enough for what he did. I seem to recall, in my day, that a little poaching wasn't unheard of after rifle drill. Nothing official, of course, but then everything isn't always done in official ways, Captain. If you take my meaning."

"I'll consider your recommendation, sir."

"Do! Do! Good night, Captain—and bon voyage."

Outside, the captain wandered about for some time to no apparent purpose. Perhaps he was considering the colonel's suggestion; more probably he was only considering the colonel. His wanderings brought him to the center of the unlighted parade grounds

He looked about him, scanning the sky—forgetting, since he had lived so many years beneath it, that this was not the real sky but a simulation; for Camp Jackson, Virginia, was nestled under the western edge of the Washington D.C. Dome. The dome was studded with millions of subminiaturized photoelectric cells which read the positions of the revolving stars and reduplicated their shifting pattern on the underside of its immense canopy.

There, low in the East, in the constellation of Taurus, was Mars—the red planet, portent of war. It was very strange; it almost exceeded belief that in less than twelve hours he, Captain Nathan Hansard of "A" Artillery Company of the Camp Jackson/Mars Command Post, would be standing with his feet firmly planted upon that speck of reddish light.

TWO

THE STEEL WOMB

It measured, on the outside, 14.14′ x 14.14′ x 10.00′, so that an observer regarding it from the floor of the hall in which it stood would see each face of it as a golden rectangle. The walls were two feet thick, of solid chrome-vanadium steel, covered with banks and boards of winking colored lights. The play of these lights, itself an imposing spectacle, was accompanied by nervous cracklings and humming sounds vaguely suggestive of electricity, or at least of Science.

There was a single opening to this sanctum—a portal some four feet in diameter set into the center of one of the golden rectangles, like the door of a bank vault. Even when this portal was open it was not possible for onlookers to glimpse the awesome central chamber itself, for a mobile steel antechamber would hide it from view at such times. No one but the men who had made the jump —the priests, as it were, of this mystery—had ever seen what it was like inside the Steel Womb.

And it was all fakery, mere public relations and stagecraft. The jump to Mars could have been made with the equivalent of four tin cans full of electronic hardware and a power source no greater than would have been available from a wall socket. The lights winked only for the benefit of the photographers from *Life*; the air hummed so that visiting Congressmen might be persuaded that the nation was getting its money's worth. The whole set had been designed not by any engineer but by Emily Golden, who had also done the sets a decade before for Kubrick's *Brave New World*.

Superfluous it might be, but it was no less daunting for all that. Hansard was given ample time to savor the spectacle. Once "A" Company had arrived at the outer, outer gate of the security complex of which the transmitter was the navel stone, there had been a continuous sorting through of passes and authorizations; there had been searches, identity checks, telephone confirmations—every imaginable kind of appetizer.

It was an hour before they reached the heart of the labyrinth, the hall that housed the Holy of Holies, and it was another hour before each man had been cleared for the jump. The hall they waited in was about as big as a small-town high-school auditorium. The walls were bare, unpainted concrete, the better to focus all eyes upon that magnificent Christmas tree at the center of the room. Large as it was, however, the hall seemed crowded now.

There were guards everywhere. There were guards before the portal of the Womb, a dozen at least; there were guards at the doubly-locked door that led out of the hall; there were guards all around the Christmas tree, like so many khaki-wrapped presents, and there were guards, seemingly, to guard the presents. There was a whole cordon of guards around the men of "A" Company, and there were also guards behind the glass partitions halfway up the walls of the hall.

It was there, in the booths behind those windows, that the technicians adjusted the multitude of dials that made the Christmas tree glow and bubble, and operated the single toggle switch that could send the contents of the transmitter from Earth to Mars in literally no time at all.

The lights were reaching their apotheosis, and the countdown had already begun for the opening of the portal (countdowns being the very stuff of drama), when the door that led into the hall opened and a two-star general under heavy guard entered and approached Hansard. Hansard recognized him from his photograph as General Foss, the chief of all Mars operations.

After the formalities of introduction and identification, General Foss explained his purpose succinctly: "You are to present this attaché case, containing a Priority-A letter, to the commanding officer, General Pittmann, immediately upon arrival. You will witness him remove the letter from the case."

"General Pittmann—the C.O.!"

General Foss made no further explanations; none were necessary, and he did not seem disposed to practice conversation for its own sake.

Hansard was embarrassed at his outburst, but he was nonetheless pleased to be enlightened. That General Pittmann was now heading the Mars Command Post explained the otherwise inexplicable fact of Hansard's transfer from the Pentagon to Camp Jackson. It was not Hansard who was being transferred so much as Pittmann; the General's aide had simply been swept up in his wake.

They might have told me, Hansard thought, though it did not surprise him that they had not. It would not have been the Army way.

Already the first squad of eight men, concealed in the belly of the mobile antechamber as in some very streamlined Trojan horse, were approaching the portal of the transmitter. The antechamber locked magnetically into place, and there was a pause while the portal opened and the eight men, all unseen, entered the Womb. Then the antechamber moved back, revealing only the closed portal.

The multitude of lights ornamenting the surface of the transmitter now darkened, with the exception of a single green globe above the portal which indicated that the eight men were still present within. The hall had grown hushed. Even the guards, themselves a part of the stage-craft, regarded this moment of the mystery with reverence.

The green light turned to red: the men were on Mars.

The Christmas tree lit up again, and the process was repeated three more times for three more squads of men. Nine, ten, even a dozen men might have occupied the inner chamber without discomfort, but there was a regulation to the effect that eight was to be the maximum number of men to be allowed in the manmitter at any one time. No one knew why such a regulation had been made, but there it was. It was now a part of the rites surrounding the mystery, and had to be observed. It was the Army way.

After the four squads had made the jump, there remained a single soldier—a Negro private whose name Hansard was uncertain of (he was either Young or Pearsall)—and Hansard himself. A warrant officer informed Hansard that he had the option of making the jump with this soldier, or going through alone afterward.

"I'll go now." It was more comfortable, in a way, to have company.

He tucked the attaché case under his arm and climbed up the ladder and into the antechamber. The private followed. They sat upon a narrow ledge and waited while the Trojan horse rolled slowly and smoothly toward the portal of the manmitter.

"Made many jumps, Private?"

"No, sir. This is the first. I'm the only one in the company that hasn't been there before."

"Not the only one, Private. It's my first jump too."

The antechamber locked against the steel wall of the transmitter, and the portal opened inward with a discreet *click*. Crouching, Hansard and the private entered. The door closed behind them.

Here there were no special effects; neither rumblings nor flashing lights. The noise in his ears was the pulse of his own blood. The feeling in his stomach was a cramped muscle. As he had done in the practice session, he stared intently at the sign stencilled with white paint on the wall of the vault:

CAMP JACKSON/EARTH
MATTER TRANSMITTER

Then, in an instant, or rather in no time at all, the sign had changed. Now it read:

CAMP JACKSON/MARS
MATTER TRANSMITTER

It was as simple as that.

The instantaneous transmission of matter, the most important innovation in the history of transportation since the wheel, was the invention of a single man, Dr. Bernard Xavier Panofsky. Born in Poland in 1929, Panofsky spent his youth and early adolescence in a Nazi labor camp where his childhood genius first manifested itself in a series of highly ingenious—and successful—escape plans. Upon being liberated, so the story goes, he immediately applied himself to the formal study of mathematics and found to his chagrin that he had, independently and all ignorantly, reinvented that branch of mathematics known as analysis situs, or topology.

In the late sixties, and already a middle-aged man, Panofsky masterminded his final escape plan: He and three confederates were the last men known to have got over the Berlin Wall. Within a year he had obtained an associate professorship in mathematics at a Catholic university in Washington D.C. By 1970 topology was an unfashionable field; even Game Theory, after a long heyday, was losing favor to the newer science of Irrationality.

In consequence, though Panofsky was one of the world's foremost topologists, the research grant that he received was trifling. In all his work, he never used a computer and never employed more than a single assistant, and even in building the pilot model of the transmitter he spent only $18,560. There wasn't a mathematician in the country who didn't agree that Panofsky's example had set the prestige of their science back fifty years.

It is an almost invariable rule that the great mathematicians have done their most original work in their youth, and Panofsky had been no exception. The theoretical basis of the transmitter had been laid as long ago as 1943, when in fashioning his own topological axioms, the fourteen-year-old prisoner naïvely evolved certain features discordant with the classical theories—chiefly the principle that became known as the Paradox of the Exploding Klein Bottle. It was to be the work of his next forty years to try to resolve these discrepancies; then, this proving impossible, to exploit them.

The first transmission was made on Christmas Day of 1983, when Panofsky transported a small silver crucifix (weight: 7.4 grams) from his laboratory on the campus to his home seven blocks away. Because of the circumstances surrounding this event, Panofsky's achievement was not given serious attention by the scientific community for almost a year. It did not help that the press insisted on speaking of the transmission as a "miracle," or that a shrewd New York entrepreneur, Max Brede (pronounced Brady), was selling replicas (in plated nickel) of the Miraculous Hopping Cross within weeks of the first newspaper stories.

But of course it was a fact, not a miracle, and facts can be verified. Quickly enough Panofsky's invention was taken seriously—and taken away. The Army, under the Emergency Allocation of Resources Act (rather hastily drawn up by Congress for the occasion) had appropriated the transmitter, despite all that Panofsky and his sponsors (which now included not only his university, but General Motors and Ford-Chrysler as well) could do. Since that time Panofsky found himself once again a prisoner, for it was obviously contrary to the nation's best interests that the mind that harbored such strategic secrets should experience all the dangers of freedom.

Like the President, and ten or twelve other "most valuable" men, Panofsky lived virtually under house arrest. To be sure, it was the most elegant of houses, having been specially constructed for him on a site facing the university campus. But the gilt of the cage did little to cheer the prisoner within, whose singular (and inadvertent) manner of escaping from these circumstances we shall have opportunity to consider later in this history.

The invention suffered a fate similar to the inventor's. The transmitters, as we have already seen, were even more fastly guarded than he and were used almost exclusively for defense purposes (though the State Department had managed to have its chief embassies provided with small, one-man models), to the despair of Panofsky and a minority of editorialists—both right and left—and to the secret relief of every major element of the economy. Understandably, the business community dreaded to think what chaos would result from the widespread use of a

23

mode of transportation that was instantaneous, weighed (in the final improved model) a mere 49½ ounces, and consumed virtually no power.

Yet even in its limited military application the transmitter had changed the face of the earth. In 1983, the year of the Miraculous Hopping Cross, the Russians had established a thriving and populous base on the moon, while the United States had twice suffered the ignominy of having lost the teams of astronauts they had tried to land in the Mare Imbrium. More than prestige was involved, for the Russians claimed to have developed a missile that could be launched from the moon with fifty per cent greater accuracy than the then presently existing ICBM's; a boast made more probable by Russia's unilateral earthside disarmament. International pressures began to mount that the United States follow suit, ignoring the fact that the Russian disarmament was more apparent than real. With the advent of the transmitter, the situation was reversed.

By 1985, thanks to its transmitters, the United States manpower on Mars exceeded Soviet lunar manpower by four hundred per cent. All American nuclear weapons were removed to the neighboring planet and by 1986 world disarmament was a fact, if not a very significant one. For the sword of Damocles was still poised above the earth, and the thread by which it hung seemed more frayed than ever.

The missiles that were stockpiled on Mars were not, strictly speaking, to be launched from that planet, but rather to be transmitted thence to satellites in permanent orbit above enemy territory; and these satellites, in turn, would relay them to their destinations. The satellites were clap-trap affairs, their only purpose being to keep aloft the 49½ ounces of receiving equipment—and a miniature radar that could trigger the self-annihilation of the receiver should any object approach it nearer than fifty feet—i.e., should the Russians try to kidnap one. Once at the satellite, each missile was programmed to home in on its target by itself.

If only the receivers could have been dispensed with!

The strategists of the Pentagon sighed for that millennial possibility, but it was not to be: all their mathematicians confirmed Panofsky's assurance that transmission could only be made from one machine *here* to another machine *there*. If the necessity for that second machine (the receiver) had not existed, anything might have been possible. Anything—but particularly a conclusive end to the Cold War. A victory! For with a means of delivering bombs *directly and instantaneously* from Mars to Russian soil . . .

From Mars? From anywhere—from the other end of the galaxy, if need be. Without the necessity of sending a receiver on ahead to one's destination, distances were meaningless. Mars could be dispensed with; the satellites could be dispensed with; in the long run, with the universe at one's disposal, even earth could probably be dispensed with.

But the receivers, alas, *were* necessary. The relay satellites were necessary. And Mars, or some such storehouse, was necessary.

And finally there was that necessity which all the other necessities took for granted—the necessity for Armageddon. Bombs, after all, are made to be dropped.

"Welcome to Mars, Nathan."

"It's good to be back, sir."

"To be—Oh, well, thank you. It's good to *have* you back. Sit down, and tell me about the trip."

General Pittmann sat down in one of two facing easy chairs, and crossed his legs so that his ankle rested on his knee. He might have been a store mannikin, so perfectly did his tailored uniform drape itself about him while preserving its immaculate crease. Perfect too were the manicured nails, the thick hair just starting to gray, the deeply tanned and artificially weathered complexion, and the unemphatic and slightly mocking smile.

"The trip was uneventful but never dull for a moment. This case, sir, contains a letter for you. Priority-A. I was instructed by General Foss to see you take it out of the case."

"Old Chatterbox Foss, eh? Here's the key, Nathan. Will you open it up for me? I've been expecting something on this order."

As General Pittmann read the letter the smile disappeared from his face and a slight frown creased his brow, but even this seemed somehow decorative. "As I feared," he said, handing the letter to Hansard, who regarded it doubtfully. "Yes, read it, Nathan. It will ease my mind if someone else knows. I'll take my chances that you're not a security risk."

The letter directed that the total nuclear arsenal of Camp Jackson/Mars be released on the enemy, who was unnamed, who did not need to be named, on the first day of June 1990, according to existing Operational Plan B. It was signed by President Lee Madigan and sealed with the Great Seal.

Hansard handed the letter back to his superior. "It hardly gives a person a chance to breathe," he commented with calculated ambiguity.

The smile ventured a tentative return. "Oh, we have six weeks of breathing—and I'm certain that before the deadline falls due the order will have been rescinded. Yes, surely it will. This is mere brinkmanship. The news of the order will be leaked through the usual channels, and the Russians will negotiate whatever issue has brought the matter up. Jamaica, I should imagine, in this case. Also, Madigan has to show he isn't soft. How will they know to dread our bombs unless we're ready to drop them? We are ready to drop them, aren't we, Nathan?"

"The command isn't mine to give, sir."

"Nor mine. It is the President's. But it *is* ours to obey. It *is* our finger, mine or yours—" As if in demonstration, Pittmann lifted a single manicured finger in the immemorial gesture of the young Baptist. "—which must be prepared to press the button. But don't you feel, for instance, that such an action would be—as I've somewhere seen it called—genocidal?"

"As you've said, sir, the whole concept of a deterrent force is valueless if we refuse to employ it."

"Which doesn't quite answer my question."

"With your permission, sir, I don't think it's my place to answer such a question."

"Nor is it, indeed, mine to ask it. You're right, Nathan. Sometimes it is the wisest course to step back from too precise a knowledge of consequences. That is part of the rationale, I'm sure, of our being on Mars and the Russians on the moon. We can take a more disinterested view out here."

"Out here . . ." Hansard echoed, gliding away from a subject he had little taste for. "It's strange, but I have no feeling yet of being out *here* at all. Camp Jackson/Mars and Camp Jackson/Virginia are so much the same."

"The sense of their difference will come all too quickly. But if you're in a hurry, you might visit the viewing dome and look out at the dust and the rocks and the dusty rocky craters. Otherwise, we have few tourist attractions here. The sense of difference lies more in the absence of earth than in the presence of the dust and rocks, as you will find. Tell me, Nathan, have you wondered why you've been chosen for this assignment?"

"As your aide, sir."

"Of course. But I had upward of a dozen aides in Washington, several of them closer than you, as chance would have it."

"Then I appreciate that you've chosen me from among them."

"It wasn't I who chose you—though I approve the choice—but the psychologists. We're here, you and I, mostly on account of our latest multiphasics—those tests we took in December with all those dirty questions. It seems we are very solid personality types."

"I'm glad to hear it."

"It hasn't always been the case with you, has it, Nathan?"

"You've seen my file, sir, so you know. But all that happened in the past. I've matured since then."

"Maturity, ah, yes. Undoubtedly we're mature enough for the work. We can do what has to be done, even if we don't quite like to give it a name."

Hansard regarded the general curiously, for his speech

was most uncharacteristic of the terran Pittmann that Hansard had known. Mars was having an effect on him.

"But all that is neither here nor there, and you must be anxious to see your quarters and look over the lovely Martian landscape. You'll be disillusioned quickly enough without my help. The great problem here is boredom. The great problem anywhere is boredom; but here it is more acute. The library is well stocked though not exactly up to the minute. The Army usually seems to regard books less than ten years old as subversive. I suggest that you try something solid and dull and very long, like *War and Peace*. No, I forgot—they don't have that here. For my own part, I've been going through Gibbon's *Decline and Fall*.

"Some day, when the time lies heavier on your hands, remind me to tell you the story of Stilicho, the barbarian who was the general of the Roman Armies. A paragon of fidelity, Stilicho. Honorius, the Emperor he served, was some kind of cretin and spent all his time breeding poultry. The Empire was falling apart at the seams; there were Goths and Vandals everywhere, and only Stilicho was holding them off. Honorius, at the instigation of a eunuch, finally had him assassinated. It was his only definitive act.

"It's a wonderful allegory. But I see you're anxious to sightsee. Officers' mess is at thirteen hundred hours. As we two are the only officers here, I shall probably see you then. And, Captain—"

"Sir?"

"There's no need for you to frown so. I assure you, it's all brinkmanship and bluff. It's happened ten times before, to my sure knowledge. In a week or two it will be all over.

"Or," the general added to himself, sotto voce, when Hansard had left the room, "in six weeks at the very limit."

THREE

THE ECHO

The antechamber locked against the steel wall of the transmitter, and the portal opened inward with a discreet *click*. Crouching, Hansard and the private entered. The door closed behind them.

Here there were no special effects; neither rumblings nor flashing lights. The noise in his ears was the pulse of his own blood. The feeling in his stomach was a cramped muscle. As he had done in the practice session, he stared intently at the sign stencilled with white paint on the wall of the vault:

CAMP JACKSON/EARTH
MATTER TRANSMITTER

For the briefest of moments he thought the EARTH had flickered to MARS, but he decided his nerves were playing tricks, for EARTH, solidly EARTH, it had remained. He waited. It should have taken only a few seconds for the technician in the glass booths outside to flick the switch that would transfer them to Mars. Hansard wondered if something had gone wrong.

"They sure do take their own sweet time," the Negro private complained.

Hansard watched as the second-hand of his wrist watch moved twice around the dial. The private seated across from him rose to his feet with an uncanny quietness and walked over to the portal, which here seemed no more than a hairline-thin circle drawn upon the solid steel. As a preventive measure against claustrophobia, however, a massive functionless doorhandle ornamented its surface.

"This son of a bitch ain't working!" the private said. "We're *stuck* in this goddamn tomb!"

"Calm down, Private—and *sit* down. You heard what

they said at the practice session about touching the walls. Keep your hand away from that handle."

But the private, thoroughly panicked, had not heard Hansard's words. "I'm getting *out* of here. I'm not gonna—"

His hand was only centimeters away from the door-handle when he saw the other hand. It was freckled and covered with a nap of red hair. It was reaching for him through the steel wall.

The private screamed and stumbled backward. Even these clumsy movements were performed with that same catlike quietness. A second disembodied hand, differing from the first in that it held a revolver, appeared. Then, bit by bit, the plane of the door surrendered the entire front of the body so that it formed a sort of bas-relief. The private continued his muted screaming.

Hansard did not at first recognize the apparition as Worsaw. Perhaps, after all, it was not Worsaw, for Hansard had seen him only minutes before, in uniform and clean-shaven—and this man, *this* Worsaw, was dressed in walking shorts and a tee-shirt and sported a full red beard.

"Hiya, Meatball," he said (and certainly it was Worsaw's voice that spoke), addressing the private, who became silent once more. "How'd you like to be integrated?" A rhetorical question, for without waiting for a reply he shot the private three times in the face. The body crumpled backward against—and partly through—the wall.

Hansard had heard of no other cases of insanity produced by transmittal, but then he knew so little about it altogether. Perhaps he was not mad, but only dreaming. Except that in dreams the dreamers should not be discountenanced by the bizarreness of the dream-world.

"That takes care of *one* son of a bitch," the spectral Worsaw said.

Before the man's murderous inference could be realized, Hansard acted. In a single motion he threw himself from the bench, and the attaché case that he had been holding at Worsaw's gun hand. The gun went off, doing harm only to the case.

In leaping from the bench, Hansard had landed on the

30

floor of the steel vault, or, more precisely, *in it,* for his hands had sunk several inches into the steel, which felt like chilled turpentine against his skin. This was strange, really very strange. But for the time being Hansard had accepted the logic of this dream-world and was not to be distracted from his immediate purpose, which was to disarm Worsaw, by any untimely sense of wonderment. He sprang up to catch hold of Worsaw's hand, but found that with the same movement his legs sank knee-deep into the insubstantial floor.

Hansard's actions would have been fatally slow, except that when the attaché case had struck Worsaw the latter staggered backward half a step. Mere inches, but far enough so that his face vanished into the wall out of which it had materialized. But the gun and the hand that held it were still within the vault and Hansard, lunging and sinking at once, caught hold of the former.

He tried to lever the weapon out of Worsaw's hand, but Worsaw held fast to it. As he struggled, Hansard found himself sinking deeper into the floor, and the drag of his weight unbalanced Worsaw. Hansard gave a violent twist to the arm of the falling man. The gun fired.

And Worsaw was dead.

Hansard, waist-deep in chrome-vanadium steel, stared at the bleeding body before him. He tried not to think, fearing that if he ventured even the smallest speculation he would lose all capacity for action. It was hard to maintain even the most provisional faith in the dream-world.

He found that if he moved slowly he was able to raise himself out of the floor, which then supported the full weight of his body in the customary manner of steel floors. He picked up the attaché case (even here in the dream-world, a Priority-A letter commands respect), and sat down carefully on the bench.

Avoiding the sight of the two corpses, he stared intently at the sign stencilled on the wall of the vault:

CAMP JACKSON/EARTH

MATTER TRANSMITTER

He counted to ten (no better strategy suggested itself), but the corpses were still there afterward; and when he poked the toe of his shoe at the floor, he punctured the steel with his foot. He was stuck in his dream.

Which was only a polite way of saying, he realized, that he was mad. But damn it, he didn't *feel* mad.

There was no time for finer flights of epistemology, for at that moment another man entered through the wall of the vault. It was Worsaw. He was barechested and wearing skivvies, and Hansard was glad to see that his hands were empty. The living Worsaw looked at the dead Worsaw on the floor and swore.

Now Hansard did panic, though in his panic he did a wiser thing than he could have conceived soberly. He ran away. He turned around on the bench where he had been sitting and ran away through the steel wall.

Coming out of the wall, he fell four feet and sank up to the middle of his calves in the concrete floor. Directly in front of him, not two feet away, was one of the M.P.'s that guarded the manmitter.

"Guard!" he shouted. "Guard, there's someone—" His voice died in his throat as the hand that he had placed upon the guard's shoulder sank through his flesh as through a light mist of sea spray. The guard gave no sign that he had felt Hansard's hand or heard his voice.

But others did—and now Hansard became aware that the hall was filled with unauthorized personnel. Some of them Hansard recognized as men from his own company, though like the two Worsaws, they were all bearded and dressed as though they were on furlough in Hawaii; others were complete strangers. They moved about the hall freely, unchallenged by the guards to whom they seemed to be invisible.

Worsaw stepped out of the steel wall behind Hansard. He was holding the gun that had belonged to his dead double. "All right, Captain, the fun's done. Now, let's see what you got in that briefcase."

Hansard broke into a sprint, but two of Worsaw's confederates blocked his path in the direction he had taken.

"Don't waste bullets, Snooky," one of these men shouted —a scrawny, towheaded man that Hansard recognized as Corporal Lesh. "We'll get him."

Hansard veered to the right, rounding the corner of the manmitter. There, in a heap before the door of the Steel Womb, were half the men of "A" Company—all eight of the Negroes and five whites—in their uniforms and either dead or dying. Nearby was another, more orderly pile of bodies; here the remaining men of the company were bound hand and foot. A second Lesh and a man unknown to Hansard stood guard over them with rifles.

Worsaw—the same Worsaw that Hansard had seen enter the manmitter with the last squad that morning—struggled to his feet and shouted, "Don't kill that bastard—you hear me? Don't touch him. I want him for myself!"

Lesh, who had been raising his rifle to take aim at Hansard, seemed uncertain whether to heed his prisoner's request or kick him back into the heap. His doubt was resolved by the other Worsaw—the Worsaw with the revolver—who commanded Lesh to do as his double (or would it be triple in this case?) had ordered. "If the fourteen of us can't take care of a goddamn fairy officer then he deserves to get away."

Hansard was encircled, and each moment the circle narrowed. He stood with his back to the wall of the transmitter (upon which the Christmas-tree lights were festively a-burble once more), and considered whether to make a dash to the right or to the left—then realized that his encirclement was only apparent, that there was a clear path to the rear.

He turned and leaped once more through the steel wall of the vault. Forgetting that the floor of the inner chamber was raised two feet above the floor level of the hall, he found himself standing knee-deep in steel again.

Like a wading pool, he thought, and the thought saved his life. For, if he could wade in it, should he not be equally able to swim in it?

Filling his lungs, he bent double and plunged his whole body into the yielding floor. With his eyes closed and the handle of the attaché case clenched between his teeth (Priority-A was, after all, the ultimate security rating), he went through the motions of swimming underwater. His limbs moved through the metamorphosed steel

33

more easily than through water, but he had no way of knowing if these motions were propelling him forward.

There was no sensation, as there would be for a swimmer, of water flowing over his skin; only a feeling through his entire body, internally as well as externally, of tingling—as though he had been dipped into a mild solution of pure electricity, if such a thing could be.

He "swam" until he was sure that, if his swimming was having any effect at all, he was out of the hall. Then he changed direction, angling to the right. At last, starved for oxygen, he had to "surface." He came up inside a broom closet. It was as good a place as any to catch his breath and gather his wits.

He rested there, only his head projecting out of the floor (his body, cradled in its substance, showed no tendencies either to rise or sink), fearful that his labored breathing might betray his presence to the . . . What *were* they—mutineers? Phantoms?

Or phantasms, the product of his own paranoia?

But he knew perfectly well that he was not mad, and if he were ever to become mad he would not have inclined in the direction of paranoia. He had taken an MMPI only last December, and Pittmann had shown him the results. It was scarcely possible to be more sane than Nathan Hansard.

In the dim light that filtered into the closet through the crack under the door Hansard could see motes of dust riding in the air. He blew at them, but his breath did not affect their demure Brownian movement. Yet he could feel the movement of that same air against his fingertip.

Conclusion? That he, and the crew that had come baying after his blood, were of another substance than the physical world they moved in. That he was, in short, a spirit. A ghost.

Was he, then, dead? No—for death, he had long ago decided, was mere insentience. Or, if he had died inside the transmitter and this *were* some sort of afterlife, the system of Dante's Inferno was evidently not going to be of any use as a guide.

Whatever had happened, happened during the time Han-

34

sard was in the transmitter. Instead of going to Mars at the moment of the jump there had been a malfunction, and his new immaterial condition (for it was simpler to assume that it was he who had changed and not the world about him) was its result.

And all the other wraiths—the three separate Worsaws, the two Leshes, the pile of corpses—were *all* of them the result of similar malfunctions? The bearded Worsaw, he who had first stepped into the vault and would now step out of it no more, was probably, by this theory, the product of some earlier transmission breakdown. But what then of the two *other* Worsaws? Where had they come from? From subsequent breakdowns, presumably.

But this would mean that the original Worsaw who had gone through the machine, the *real* Worsaw, had continued the course of his own life in the real world, served his term of duty on Mars and returned to earth—and made the Mars jump again. Twice again, counting today's jump. And this *real* Worsaw went on with his life in complete ignorance of the existence of the *Doppelgängers* splitting off from him. And if all this were true . . .

Then there would also be another Nathan Hansard on the Mars Command Post, of whom he—the Nathan Hansard resting in the concrete floor of the broom closet—was a mere carbon copy resulting from the imperfect operation of the transmitter.

Though for all he knew, this was its normal function.

In support of his theory, Hansard recollected that there had been a moment within the transmitter when he had thought he'd seen the word EARTH flicker to MARS. *Had* he made the jump to Mars and then bounced back like a rubber ball in that briefest of moments when the operating switch was flicked on?

Like a rubber ball, or like . . . an echo. . . .

But this was not the time or the place to elaborate ingenious theories. Worsaw and his confederates were undoubtedly searching the building and the grounds for him at this moment. He ducked back beneath the floor and "swam" on through the foundations, surfacing only for air or to get his bearings; now bobbing up into an office full of silent, industrious clerks (for there were no noises in this dream-world except the sound of his own breathing), then into an empty corridor or an unfurnished room (with which the building seemed to abound, like some gigantic coral reef). It was several minutes before he was outside the labyrinth of the security complex and in the sunlight of the April noonday where he saw, but was not seen by, two of Worsaw's bearded friends.

It would not do to remain in Camp Jackson. He had lost the cap of his uniform in the transmitter, or in his flight from the hall, so that he would be conspicuously out of uniform here. Among the throngs of the city, however, he would be as good as invisible, because if he refrained from walking through walls there would be no visual evidence of his dematerialized state.

He considered how he could travel the ten miles to downtown D.C. most quickly. *Not* by swimming. Ordinarily he would have taken the bus. . . .

It felt strange to pass out the gate of Camp Jackson without showing a pass or I-D. The city-bound bus was waiting at the curb. Hansard got on, careful to walk lightly so that his feet would not pass through the floor, and took an empty seat by a window. A moment later a private sat down in the same seat—*and in Hansard.* Hansard, much shaken, moved to the seat across the aisle.

The bus started up slowly, and Hansard was able to keep from sinking all the way through his seat. Each time the bus accelerated or decelerated Hansard was in danger of slipping out of the vehicle altogether. At a traffic light just before the bridge over the Potomac the bus braked suddenly and Hansard somersaulted through the seat in front of him, down through the floor of the bus and the transmission, and deep into the roadway itself.

After that he decided to hike the rest of the way into the city.

FOUR

THE REAL WORLD

In witnessing the foregoing remarkable events, it may have occurred to the reader to wonder how he would have reacted in Hansard's circumstances, and if this reader were of a skeptical temperament he might very well question the plausibility of Hansard's so-sudden and so-apt adjustment to the enormous changes in the world about him. Yet this hypothetical skeptic shows the same ready adaptibility every night in his dreams.

Hansard, in those first perilous minutes, was living in a dream, and his actions showed the directness and simplicity of the actions of a dreamer. What had he done, after all, but flee from the face of danger? It can be objected that Hansard was *not* dreaming; but can we be so sure of that yet? When else, in the usual course of experience, does one walk through steel walls?

So it is not really so wonderful that Hansard should have fallen into a half-dreaming state and been able to act so naturally amid so much that was unnatural. Perhaps our skeptical reader might even allow that, with the wind in the right direction, he might not have acted entirely differently himself—at least he should not discount the possibility.

Hansard did not shake off this sense of unreality at once. Indeed, with the occasion for action past, with nothing to do but explore and reflect, this sense grew, and with its growth he felt the beginnings of dread—of a subtle terror worse than anything he had experienced in the hall outside the transmitter. For it is possible to flee the figures of a nightmare, but there is no escape from the nightmare itself but waking.

The worst of it was that none of the people that he passed on the city streets, the drivers of cars and buses, the clerks in stores, *no one* would look at him. They disregarded Hansard with an indifference worthy of gods. Hansard stood between the jeweler and his lamp, but the wraith's shadow was as imperceptible to the jeweler as was the wraith himself. Hansard grasped the diamond in his own hand; the jeweler continued his careful cutting. Once, when he was crossing a street, a truck turned the corner and without even ruffling Hansard's hair drove straight through him.

It was as though he were a beggar or deformed, but in that case they would at least have looked away, which was some sort of recognition. No, it was as though each one of them had said to him: *You do not exist,* and it became increasingly difficult not to believe them.

So that Hansard walked through this unheeding, intangible city as through a dream-landscape, observing but not understanding it, not even endeavoring as yet to understand it. He walked past the immemorial, unmemorable white stoneheaps of the capital buildings: the unfenestrated mausoleum that housed the National Gallery; the monumental Yawn of the Supreme Court; the Capitol's Great White Wart; and that supreme dullness, the Washington Monument.

Though he had lived in the District of Columbia for the last eight years, though he had passed these buildings almost daily, though he even supposed that he admired them, he had never *seen* them before. He had always regarded them with the same unseeing, reverential eyes with which he would have regarded, for instance, his nation's flag.

But now, curiously (for architecture was far from being his immediate concern), he saw them as they were, with the veil of the commonplace ripped away. Why, he wondered, did the capitals of the columns burst into those Corinthian bouquets? Why, for that matter, were the columns there? Everything about these buildings seemed arbitrary, puzzling. Presumably they had been built for human purposes—but what purpose can be served by a five-hundred-fifty-five-foot obelisk?

He stood beneath the blossoming, odorless cherry trees and tried to argue against the horror mounting within him.

38

At those rare moments when the skin of the world is peeled away and its substance laid bare before us, the world may assume either of two aspects—benign or malignant. There are those sublime, Wordsworthian moments when Nature apparels herself in celestial light; but there are other moments too, when, with the same trembling sensibility and the same incontrovertible sureness, we see that the fair surface of things—all flesh, these white and scentless blossoms, the rippled surface of the reflecting pool, even the proud sun itself—are but the whiting on the sepulchre within which . . . it were best not to look.

Hansard stood at such a brink that first afternoon, and then he drew back. Once already in his life, long ago and in another country, he had stepped beyond that threshold and let himself see what lay there, so that this time he was able to foresee well in advance that such a moment threatened again. (The symptoms were clear. A minacious cold seemed to settle over him, followed by a feeling of hollowness that, originating in the pit of his stomach, spread slowly to all his limbs; his thoughts, like the music on a record placed off-center on a turntable, moved through his consciousness at eccentric tempi—now too fast and now too slow.)

He foresaw what was to be, and resisted it. This is not an easy thing to do. Most of us are passive before our strongest emotions, as before one of the Olympian gods. Even Medusa-headed horror has an allure, though we won't often admit it; and when we do surrender ourselves to her it is with averted eyes and the pretence that we are not helping out.

The same reader who may at first have tended to overvalue Hansard's quick reflexes in the face of immediate danger may now be inclined to value his struggle with the "Medusa" too lightly, or not at all. Let such a reader be assured of the reality of this peril. Had Hansard succumbed to these feelings—had he, slipping into solipsism, let himself believe that the Real World was not any longer as real as it had been, then we would either have a much shorter and sadder tale to tell, or we would have had to find another hero for it.

39

But for all that, it is true that a man in good health can bear a few hours of supernatural terror without lasting ill effect. The worst fear, after all, is of the known rather than of the unknown—a truth that Hansard became aware of as soon as he realized, about sunset, that the hollow feeling in the pit of his stomach was a symptom of more than malaise; it was simply hunger pangs. And worse than the hunger pangs was his thirst.

In restaurants he could see people eating, but their food —like all matter that belonged exclusively to the Real World—sifted through his fingers like vapor. He could not turn on a water faucet or lift a glass, and if he could have it would have availed him nothing, for the water of the Real World was as insubstantial as its solid matter. Hansard stood in a public fountain and let the water cascade through his body without dampening his clothes, or his thirst. It began to seem that his sojourn in the dream-world might not be of much longer duration than a dream. How long could one go without food or water? Three days? Four?

But what then of Worsaw and the others in Camp Jackson? To judge only by the length of their beards these men were veterans of the dream-world, from which it was only reasonable to suppose that some place in this city there was ghostly food and drink to satisfy his most unghostly appetites. He had only to find it.

If the theory he had developed earlier that day concerning the cause of his changed condition were correct, there could be but one source of the food that sustained Worsaw and Co.:—it had to originate from a transmitter, just as they themselves had. The "ghost" of food that had been transmitted to Mars would logically be the only food a ghost could eat; the "ghost" of water would be the only water a ghost could drink.

And would not the same hold true of air as well? Did Hansard breathe the same air that the residents of the Real World breathed—or another air, the "ghost" of theirs? If the latter were the case, it would explain the strange silence of the dream-world in which the only noises audible to Hansard were the noises he made himself; and

40

these, in turn, were inaudible in the Real World. The air that bore the sound waves Hansard produced was a different medium from the air of the Real World.

It was a theory easily confirmed or disproved. The transmitters that supplied the Mars Command Post with a constant fresh supply of both air and water were located beneath the D.C. Dome, just outside the eastern perimeter of Camp Jackson itself.

As the simulated daylight of the domed city modulated from dusk to darkness, Hansard walked back toward Camp Jackson on the delicate snowcrust of the sidewalks, occasionally popping his toes through the thin membrane of the surface. He had discarded his military hat and jacket, depositing them with his attaché case inside the thick walls of the Lincoln Memorial where, invisible to all eyes, Hansard was certain a Top-Priority secrecy could be preserved indefinitely. His tie was loosened, and his shirt open at the collar, despite the discomfort this caused him. Except for the officer's stripe down his pants' leg, he should pass for a pedestrian of the Real World—or so he hoped.

Hansard arrived at the barricade about the Mars "pipelines" an hour after the false twilight of the domed city had dimmed to extinction. The D.C. Dome was composed of two shells: the inner was an energy-screen, designed late in the 1970's as a defense against the neutron bombs. Had it ever been put to the test, the unhappy residents of the city would have found it no more effective a defense than a magic pentagram drawn with the fat of a hanged man—an awesome but empty symbol. Subsequent to its erection, however, this energy dome was found to have the pragmatic property of supporting a second outer dome, or skin, of plastic. Soon, from this single phenomenon, an entire technology had developed, and now it was possible to build outer domes substantial enough to act as a weather shield over areas twelve miles in diameter and able to support a complex of lighting and ventilation systems as well.

The Mars pumps stood just outside Camp Jackson, since they were officially administered by NASA, though in fact by the Army. Accordingly, Army guards patrolled the barrier built about the pumping stations. Hansard need take no heed of either guards or barrier, but he did. If his theory was correct, he would have to be wary not to encounter any other men of "A" Company, for this would be their only source of water as well as Hansard's.

Within the barrier, the grounds sloping up to the concrete pumphouse were attractively landscaped—apparently for the benefit of the inner guards, since the barrier prevented anyone else from seeing them. Hansard lowered himself into the earth and swam slowly up the hill through lawn and flowerbeds.

Reaching the pumphouse and having satisfied himself that he was alone, Hansard again assumed a standing posture and walked through the concrete wall of the building.

And found himself drowning.

The entire pumphouse was filled with water—real liquid water, or rather, unreal water of the sort that an unreal Hansard might either drink or drown in. Instead of floundering back through the wall, Hansard swam upward. The water rose to a height of fourteen feet, which was yet a few feet less than the high ceiling of the building. Surfacing, Hansard's ears popped.

The surface of the water was brightly lighted by the illuminated panels of the ceiling, and Hansard could see that the water in the center of this strange reservoir was bubbling furiously. Remarkable as these phenomena were, Hansard's first consideration was to quench his thirst and be gone. He could fit these facts to his theories at his leisure.

Regretful that he could carry back no water to the city, except what was sloshing about in the toes of his shoes, Hansard returned on the bus—this time without mischance. He got off outside the New St. George, a hotel which, in the ordinary scheme of things, he would have never been able to afford. At the reception desk he informed himself of the number of an unoccupied suite, and found his way to it up the stairs (he suspected that the hotel's elevators would start and stop too quickly for him to be able to keep from popping out through the floor).

Once in possession of his rooms he realized that he might just as well have gone to a flophouse, for he was unable to turn on the light switch. Shivering in his damp clothes, he went to sleep in the midst of the suite's undoubtable, but darkened, luxury. He slept on a canopied bed, but he would have been just as comfortable, after all, on the floor.

He woke with a bad head-cold and screaming.

It had been so many years since he had had the dream that he had been able to convince himself that he had rid himself of it. The dream always concluded with the same image, but it might begin in a variety of ways. For instance:

He was there. Drenched. Mud up to his thighs. A buzzing somewhere, always a buzzing. Always wet. Always knowing that the enveloping greenness was made green by wishing for his death. Always bodies, scrap-heaps of bodies along the muddy road. He was very young. He didn't always want to look. "I won't look," he said. Whenever he was there, in that country in his dreams, he knew how young he was. But you could look at anything if you had to. And diseases, lots of diseases. And always something that buzzed.

The people of that country were very little. Little adults, like the children in the paintings of the Colonial period. Their faces were children's faces. He could see long rows of their faces pressed up against the wire. He was carrying pots of cooked rice. When they spoke it sounded more like screaming than speech. The compound always got fuller. Every part of the fence was filled with their faces. They asked for "incendigel," which seemed to be the word for rice in their country.

This part of the dream could never have happened, he knew, except in the unreal world of dreaming, because an officer would not have carried the pots of rice himself. A private would have done that. But in the dream it was always Hansard who carried the pots of

43

incendigel and the little people stared at him hungrily, wishing for his death.

It was not a credible world; not in the sense that, for instance, Milwaukee or Los Angeles was real and credible. It was a dream-world of little half-people who could not speak unless they screamed.

And there was a lady in the middle of the road with most of her head missing. The medic cut open her belly and took out the baby. "It's going to live," he said.

"Thank God," said Hansard.

"Burn it all down," said the captain. The little men behind the wire fence began screaming when the interpreter told them what the captain was saying. They tried to get out, and the captain had to use tear gas, though he didn't want to, since supplies were limited this far inland.

He was there, in the fields. It was a hot and windless noonday. The grains were swollen with their ripeness. The flame throwers made a buzzing sound. Far across the blackened field a small figure waved at Hansard as though in greeting. "Welcome, welcome," he was screaming in his strange language.

He was screaming. He found that he had fallen through the bed. He was looking up into the bedsprings. He stopped screaming and clambered up through the mattress into daylight.

"I've stopped dreaming," he said aloud. "That was all a dream, it never happened." Though this was not strictly true, it helped him to hear himself say it. "And now it's all over, and I'm back in the Real World."

But despite these reassurances, and the good advice implicit in them that he should turn to daylight matters now, he could not keep from remembering that one moment of the dream—when he had been looking out through the wire fence at Captain Hansard carrying that big pot of rice. His mouth watered. He was hungry. He was so hungry—and he had no food.

FIVE

THE VOYEUR

One of the minor provisions of the Emergency Allocation of Resources Act had been that the various transmitters built by the government were to be situated in different states. As soon as the first receiver had made the long rocket journey to Mars and landed, materials for the construction of the Command Posts (of which there were six) were transmitted from Texas, California, and Ohio. Camp Jackson/Virginia, because it was under the D.C. Dome, was an obvious choice for the location of the one transmitter through which the personnel staffing the Command Posts was provided. Food, nonperishable goods, and artillery, however, were still supplied through the California and Ohio transmitters.

It would have been a simple enough matter to stow away in the back of a Real World truck or train bound from Washington to Cincinnati. But it was certain that if he did he would arrive in a severe, not to say fatal, state of anoxic anoxemia. For the air that Hansard breathed here in the city was not the air of the Real World, but the dematerialized air created by the transmitters and kept from dispersing by the dome above the city. Outside the dome, on the open highway or in another city, his store of dematerialized oxygen would be quickly dissipated. The dome kept him alive—but it also kept him a prisoner.

Yet there had to be food of some sort coming through the transmitters, for the men of Camp Jackson were surely sustained by more than air and water. And since the greatest aid to solving a problem is knowing that it can be solved, Hansard need not and did not panic.

Whatever food they were eating had to be going through the Camp Jackson transmitter; and as only personnel went through the transmitters it must be that the men were bringing food with them to Mars, probably concealed in their duffels. Though this was against regulations it was commonplace practice, since the Command Post lacked a PX. But how could they know to bring *enough?*

Unless there was a way, which Hansard had yet to discover, of communicating with the inhabitants of the Real World. . . .

Reluctant to return to Camp Jackson during the day, Hansard thought of some other way to put the day to good use. He remembered that the State Department had been provided with a small manmitter by which they were able to transport personnel to overseas embassies. If anyone were to go through this manmitter today, it would be well for Hansard to be on hand: Hansard could gain an ally for himself, and the new ghost would be spared considerable anguish in learning to cope with his changed condition.

It would be too much to hope that the possible State Department traveller would be bringing food with him. Nevertheless, Hansard hoped just that.

As he went out of the New St. George, Hansard stepped at the cashier's box and made out a personal check in the amount of $50.00, which he placed in the hotel's locked safe. It was not a wholly whimsical gesture, for Hansard had a highly developed conscience and he would have suffered a pang of guilt if he skipped out on a hotel bill.

He did not know in which of the several State Department buildings the small manmitter would be located, but it was a simple matter to find it by searching through the various corridors for heavy concentrations of armed guards. When he did find it, at four in the afternoon, it was immediately apparent that he had not been the first to search it out.

The walls and floor of the small anteroom adjoining the manmitter were covered with delicate traceries of dried blood, which no cleaning woman would ever remove, for they were not of the Real World. When Hansard touched a fingertip to one of these stains, the thin film crumbled into a fine powder, like ancient lace. There had been murders here, and Hansard was certain that he knew the identity of the murderers.

And the victims? He hesitated to think of what distinguished men had used the State Department's manmitter during recent months. Had not even the then Vice-President Madigan traveled to King Charles III's Coronation via this manmitter?

Hansard, absorbed in these somber considerations, was startled by the sudden flash of red above the door of the manmitter's receiver compartment, indicating that a reception had just been completed. There was a flurry of activity among the guards in the anteroom, of whose presence Hansard had been scarcely aware till then.

The door of the manmitter opened and a strange couple came out: an old man in a power wheel chair, and an attractive black-haired woman in her early thirties. Both wore heavy fur coats and caps that were matted with rain. A guardsman approached the old man and seemed to engage him in an argument.

If only I knew how to lip-read, Hansard thought, not for the first time.

His attention had been so caught up by this scene that he was not at once aware of the voices approaching the anteroom in the outer corridor. Voices . . . it could only be . . .

Hansard dodged first behind the couple in fur coats, then surveyed the room for a vantage point from which he could eavesdrop without being seen. The guard who was addressing the man in the wheel chair had been sitting at a desk, and by this desk stood a wastebasket. From the center of the room the contents of the wastebasket would be invisible.

Hansard lowered himself into the floor, careful not to allow his body to slip through the ceiling of the room immediately below, for it was only so, immersed in the "material" of the Real World, that gravity seemed to lose its hold on him. At last he was totally enveloped except for his head, which was out of sight in the waste-

47

basket. And none too soon, for by the sudden clarity of the intruders' voices Hansard knew he was no longer alone in the room.

"I told you this would be a waste of time," said a voice that seemed tantalizingly familiar. Worsaw's? No, though it had something of the same southern softness to it.

A second voice that could have belonged only to the Arkansan Lesh whined a torpid stream of obscenities in reply to the first speaker, to the general effect that he, being of a wholly inferior nature, should shut up.

A third speaker agreed with this estimate and expanded on it; he suggested that the first speaker owed himself and Lesh an apology.

"I apologize, I apologize."

"You apologize, *sir*."

"I apologize, sir," the first voice echoed miserably.

"You're goddamn right, and you'd just better remember it too. We don't *have* to keep you alive, you know. Any time I like I can just saw your fat head off, you son of a bitch, and if it wasn't for Worsaw I'd of done it long ago. I should smash your face in right now, that's what I should do."

"Ah, Lesh," said the third speaker, "don't you ever get tired of that crap? What time is it, anyhow?"

The first voice, which Hansard could still not place, said, "The clock over the desk says four-fifteen. And that means that Greenwich Mean Time is ten-fifteen, and so all the embassies in Europe are shutting down. There may still be a few people left, like that old cripple and the piece, coming back *here*. But that isn't going to do *us* any good."

"You think you're pretty goddamn smart, don't you?" Lesh whined.

"There's probably something to what he says though," the third voice put in. "There ain't any point sitting around here if nobody else is going through. Leastwise, *I* got better things to do."

Lesh, after more obscenities, agreed. Their voices faded as they left the room.

Hansard decided to follow them. He risked little in doing

so, for in his present state concealment took little effort and escape perhaps less. He dropped through the floor into the room below, and the momentum took him through the floor of that room in turn, and so on into the basement. This method of descent allowed him time to be outside the building and hidden from sight before the three men had exited from the front door.

The man whose voice had seemed familiar to Hansard walked behind the other two (who carried rifles), and was bent under the weight of a field pack so that it was not possible to see his face. The two armed men mounted a Camp Jackson-bound bus, leaving their companion to continue the journey on foot, for with the added weight of the pack and the consequent increase in momentum he would probably not have been able to stay inside the vehicle.

When the bus was out of sight, however, this figure removed his back pack and laid it in the middle of a shrub, then turned down a street in a direction that carried him away from Camp Jackson.

A canteen swung from his cartridge belt. Hansard needed that canteen for himself. He removed the field pack from the shrubbery and "buried" it hastily in the sidewalk, then set off after the vanishing figure in a soundless pantomime of pursuit: a lion padding after an inaudible quarry through a silent jungle.

After several turnings, they entered an area of luxury apartment buildings. The figure turned in at the main entrance of one of these buildings. Hansard, reluctant to follow him inside (for he might have joined more of his confederates within), waited in the doorway of the building opposite. An hour passed.

With misgivings—for he had never till now intruded upon the private lives of dwellers in the Real World—Hansard began his own exploration of the building, starting at the top floor and working his way down through the ceilings. He encountered families at dinner, or stupefied before the television; witnessed soundless quarrels, and surprised people in yet more private moments. A suspicion of his quarry's intent in coming here grew in Hansard's mind, and in Apartment 4-E this suspicion was confirmed.

Hansard found him in the apartment of an attractive and evidently newlywed couple. In the twilit room, the man was sitting upon their bed and pretending to guide, with his intangible touch, the most intimate motions of their love. While the voyeur's attention was thus directed toward the lovers Hansard approached him from behind, slipped his tie around the man's throat and tightened the slip-knot. The voyeur fell backward off the bed, and Hansard saw now for the first time who his enemy had been—Colonel Willard Ives.

Hansard dragged Ives, choking, out of the bedroom. He wrested away the man's canteen and drank greedily from it. He had been all day without water.

While Hansard was drinking from the canteen the colonel attempted to escape. Two evenings ago, in Ives's office, it would have been unthinkable that he should ever have occasion to assault his superior officer. But now the circumstances were exceptional, and Hansard performed that unthinkable action with scarcely a scruple. Afterward he gave Ives his handkerchief to stop the bleeding of his nose.

"I'll have you court-marshaled for this," Ives snuffled, without much conviction. "I'll see that you—I'll teach you to—"

Hansard, whose character had been made somewhat unpliable by fourteen years of military life, was not without retroactive qualms. "Accept my apologies, Colonel. But I can hardly be expected to regard you in the light of my superior at the moment—when I see you obeying the orders of a corporal."

Ives looked up, eyes wide with emotion. "You called me *Colonel*. Then, you know me . . . back there?"

"I was talking with you in your office only two nights ago, Colonel. Surely you remember?"

"No. No, not with me." Ives bit his lower lip, and Hansard realized that this was not, in fact, the same man. This Ives was a good seventy-five pounds lighter than his double in the Real World, and there were innumerable other details—the shaggy hair, the darker complexion, the

50

cringing manner—that showed him to be much changed from his old (or would it be his other?) self. "*I* was never a colonel. I was only a major when I went through the manmitter two years ago. Sometimes he brings me to my office—to the Colonel's office—and humiliates me there, in front of him. That's the only reason he wants me alive —so he can humiliate me. Starve me and humiliate me. If I had any courage, I'd . . . I'd . . . kill myself. I would. I'd go outside the dome . . . and . . ." Choking with pity for himself, he was obliged to stop speaking.

"He?" Hansard asked.

"Worsaw. The one you killed in the manmitter. I wish you'd killed all three of him, instead of just the one."

"How many men—of our sort—are there in Camp Jackson?"

Ives turned his gaze away from Hansard's. "I don't know."

"Colonel—or Major, if you prefer—I should not like to hurt you again."

"Wouldn't you? I doubt that. You're just the same as Worsaw. You're all the same, all of you. As soon as the discipline is gone you lose all sense of what's right and decent. You betray your allegiance. You murder and rape. You act like . . . like jungle savages. All of you."

"It doesn't seem to me, Major, that you're in a good position to offer moral instruction. Let me repeat my question: How many—"

"Seventeen, twenty, twenty-four—the number varies. Oh, you think you're so fine and upstanding, don't you! So damn *white!* They always do when they're new *here*, before they've had to . . . had to eat their . . ." He trailed off into vacancy.

"What, Major? What is it you eat here? Where do you get your food?"

Ives' eyes dropped in a mockery of shyness to contemplate the buttons on Hansard's shirt. His smile twisted with a slight, enigmatic contempt for the man who held him prisoner. It was, in fact, the characteristic smile of a prisoner who, though powerless, knows what dis-

51

tance separates himself, exalted in his guilt, from the common run.

With horror Hansard realized what the men of Camp Jackson were living on. His horror was all the more potent because he also knew that this realization had been with him from the first moment he had seen the pile of corpses outside the portal of the manmitter. For he had assessed the situation correctly. All the food that sustained Worsaw and his men would have to have come to them through the transmitter.

He knew this, yet even now he refused to believe it. "Then all those men who went through the transmitter, *all* of them . . ."

"Those niggers, you mean? You're a Northerner, aren't you, Captain? Only a Northerner would call a bunch of niggers men."

"You foulness! You corruption!"

"You wait, Captain—wait till you get hungry enough. You talk about us now, but just wait. Worsaw was the one who saw the way it had to be. He had the strength . . . and the . . . and the foresight to do what had to be done. So that we got the niggers and the nigger-lovers before they got *us*. He's kept us alive here. No one else was able to; only Worsaw. I was . . . afraid to face facts; but Worsaw went right ahead and did it. He's a . . ." the colonel began to choke again but finished his testimonial first, ". . . a good man."

"I recall that you said the same thing when last we met." Hansard rose to his feet.

"Where are you going?" Ives asked anxiously. "You won't tell *him* what I've been telling you? I'm not supposed to be here. I—"

"I'm hardly likely to have many conversations with your master, Ives. I'm going now, but you just stay here or go back in the bedroom, if you like, and wallow in your filth. As long as you can't infect *them,* it can't matter."

Hansard was at the door when Ives called him in a strangely muffled tone. Hansard looked back. Ives was sitting on the floor, his face buried in his hands.

"Captain, please! I beg of you, Captain! Do this one

52

thing—do it, I beg of you. I don't have the strength myself, but *you* could. Oh, for the love of God, *please!*"

"You want me to kill you—is that it, Major?"

"Yes," Ives whispered into his hands, "oh, yes."

"You can go to hell, Major, but it will have to be under
your own steam."

When Hansard left him, Ives was crying.

He proceeded back immediately to where he had hidden
Ives' field pack. He pulled it out of the sidewalk; then, in
the pool of light beneath a street lamp, he unbuckled it.
The flesh that still adhered to the gnawed bones had a
slightly carrion odor. Hansard dumped the charry remains into the ground and pushed them down beyond
arm's reach. At the bottom of the pack there was a .45
automatic pistol and ammunition, wrapped in a plastic
poncho. This Hansard kept for himself.

It was after sunset, time to return to the reservoir and
fill his canteen. But when he began walking his legs
betrayed him and he had to sit down. Likewise, his
hands, as he put a clip of ammunition into the automatic,
were trembling.

He was not terrified that the men at Camp Jackson
would get him; he was confident that he could prevent
that. He *was* terrified that he might get one of them—once
he was hungry enough. And then? How much farther was
it possible to sink then? He might have asked Ives while
he had the chance.

SCENE WITH A SMALL BOY

For a while food and sleep can replace each other.
Knowing this, Hansard refrained from purposeless activ-
ities; went on no more idle walks, and found a residence for himself on the Virginia side of the Potomac
nearer to his water supply. After his encounter with Ives

the idea of intruding upon the privacy of residents of the Real World was more than ever distasteful to him. On the other hand he valued his own privacy and did not want to make his home in a public concourse.

The Arlington Public Library provided a happy compromise. When people were there they behaved sedately. It was open evenings, so Hansard did not have to spend the time after sunset in darkness; even the silence of this world, so unnatural elsewhere, seemed fitting here.

At such times as Hansard could no longer pretend to himself that he was asleep (he had made the basement stacks his special burrow), he could come upstairs and read over the shoulders of whoever was in the library that day; fragments and snippets of a variety of things, as Providence saw fit to furnish: The College Outline synopses of *A Farewell to Arms, Light in August,* and diverse other Great Old Novels that were required reading in the Arlington high schools; paradigms of Bantu verbs; backnumber spools of the *Washington Post*; articles on how to develop hard, manly arms; on how to retire gracefully; on how to synthesize potatoes; and several graceful anecdotes from the lives of Christopher Robin and Pooh Bear. . . .

It was a mistake to go into the children's room and read the Milne book, for it opened his heart wide to the temptation he had all this while been strong enough to ignore. His ex-wife and son lived beneath the D.C. Dome. He could visit them with no more effort than it would take to get on an S-S-bound bus.

Since the divorce she had managed to make do on her meager alimony by moving into government-subsidized Sargent Shriver Manors, popularly known as the S-S, a model development of the early 70's and now the city's most venerable slum. (*Really* poor people, of course, had to squat out in the suburbs, breathing the poisonous air of the megalopolitan landscape.) Hansard had been able to see his son, who was now eight years old, one week end each month. But there had always been a constraint between father and son since the divorce, and Hansard still tended to think of Nathan Junior as the insouciant, golden-haired four-year-old who had listened with solemn attention to the adventures of Winnie the Pooh.

The present Nathan Junior was, therefore, in his father's eyes something of a usurper—with very tenuous claims to the title of true son or to Hansard's affection. An injustice, surely, but an injustice that no amount of fair treatment could expunge: the heart listens to no reasons but its own.

With Ives's example before him, Hansard should have known better than to surrender to this temptation. *Only a glimpse,* he told himself. *I won't look at anything they wouldn't want me to see.* Could he really deceive himself so far as to credit these sophistries? Apparently not, for as the bus was passing near the Washington Monument Hansard had second thoughts and dismounted.

He walked along the edge of the reflecting pool. He had grown so accustomed to his altered condition that, as he debated with himself, he did not dodge the lower branches of the cherry trees but passed through them unheedingly. He knew better than to believe the tempter's whispered *"Just this once."* No; there would be a second time, if he let there be a first—and a third time, and more. There is no food that can sate curiosity.

Curiosity?—the tempter argued. *Merely that? Isn't there love in it too?*

Love is reciprocal, the conscientious Hansard replied. *What has a phantom like me to do with love? And besides* (and this was the crux of it) *there is no love there any more.*

It can be seen that the debate had insensibly shifted its focus from Nathan Junior to Marion, and the tempter cleverly pointed this out. *Don't go for her sake then, but for his. It is your duty as a father.*

The tempter's arguments became weaker and weaker, his true purpose more transparent. Hansard would surely have resisted, had not a curious thing happened at that moment. . . .

Across the reflecting pool he saw, among the many tourists and lunch-hour strollers, a woman—and this

55

woman seemed for a moment to have been looking at him. She was a handsome woman about Marion's age and, like Marion, a blonde. It was impossible, of course, that she had seen him; but for a moment he had been able to believe it. He strode up to the edge of the pool (but there he had to stop, for the water of the Real World did not sustain a swimmer's weight as the land would), and called to her: "Hello, there! Hello! Can you see me? Wait— listen! No, no, stay a while!" But already she had turned away and was walking toward the Capitol and out of sight.

Then Hansard knew that despite all his good resolves he would become, like that man he had so much detested, a voyeur. He would trespass against his wife's and son's privacy. For it was not within him, nor would it be within any of us, to endure the unrelenting terror of his perfect isolation and aloneness amid the throngs of that city where every unseeing pair of eyes was a denial of his existence. If that seems to overstate the case, then instead of aloneness let us say alienation. We will all agree that there is little chance of coping with *that*.

We have observed earlier that Hansard was very little a man of his own times, and that even in ours he would have seemed rather out of date. Alienation, therefore, was for him a thoroughly unfamiliar experience, though the word had been dinned into his ears in every humanities course he'd ever taken (which had been as few as possible). So that, despite a well-developed conscience of the old-fashioned post-Puritan sort, he was singularly ill-equipped to handle his new emotions. The bottom seemed to be dropping out, as though existence had been a hangman's trap which now was sprung. He felt a hollowness at the core of his being; he felt a malaise; he felt curiously will-less, as though he had just discovered himself to be an automaton as, in a sense, he had.

In his innocence he showed symptoms of classic simplicity, like the dreams of some forest- or mountain-dweller, someone far beyond the pale who has escaped even the mention of Freud's name. There is no need to go into great detail here, except to remind the knowing reader that although Hansard experienced his first bout of the *nausée* at a rather advanced age (for the unfortunate experience that had required his presence some years before in an Army mental hospital could not fairly have been said to be "alienation" in the sense we employ here), it was no less devastating. Indeed, as is so often the case when an adult comes down with a childhood disease, it was rather worse.

The practical consequence was that he got back on the bus, but not without first resorting to his cache in the wall of the Lincoln Memorial and taking out the jacket of his uniform. Then, replacing the attaché case in the wall and very carefully straightening his tie (his concern with a good appearance was proportional to his intent to do wrong), he set off . . . downward.

She was sprawled on the living-room tuckaway—the tuckaway that had been their wedding gift from his parents—smoking and reading a personalized novel (in which the heroine was given the reader's own name). She had let herself grow heavier. It is true that a certain degree of stoutness had been fashionable for the last two years. Even so, she was beginning to exceed that certain limit. Her elaborate hairdo was preserved inviolate in a large pink plastic bubble.

There was a man in the room, but he paid little attention to Marion and she as little to him. His hairdo was likewise protected by a bubble (his was black), and his face was smeared with a cream that would give it that "smooth, leathery look" that was so much admired this year. A typical welfare dandy. He was performing isometric exercises in a kimono that Hansard had brought back from Saigon for Marion, who had then been his fiancée.

The surprising thing was that Hansard was not jealous. A little taken aback, perhaps, a little disapproving; but his disapproval was more of her generally lax style of living than of another man's presence. Adultery he could not countenance (and, in fact, he *had* not). But now Marion was free to do as she liked, within the limits of what was commonly accepted.

Love? Had he, so short a time as four years ago, loved this woman? How can emotion vanish so utterly that even its memory is gone?

Marion rose from the tuckaway and went to the door to press the buzzer opening the downstairs entry (her apartment was on 28), then disappeared into the kitchen. She had left her book open on the table beside the couch, and Hansard bent over to read a passage from it:

Marion Hansard, sitting up on the bed, glanced into the mirror of the vanity. There were times, and this one of them, when Marion was startled by her own beauty. Usually she didn't think of herself as especially attractive, though she had never been and never would be drab. But how could Marion Hansard hope to compete with the dark-eyed beauties of Mexico City, with their raven hair and haughty, sensual expressions . . . ?

Hansard looked away from his ex-wife's romance with the same embarrassment he would have felt had he walked in upon her in the performance of a shameful act. He made up his mind to leave the apartment.

Then his son came into the room.

It must have been to let him in that Marion had risen from the couch. His hair was darker than Hansard remembered, and he had lost another milk tooth. Also, he was dressed more poorly than when he went for a week-end expedition with his father.

The man in the black hair-bubble spoke to Nathan Junior in an equable manner, and Hansard was more than ever assured that he enjoyed resident status in his ex-wife's apartment. Marion returned from the kitchen and also addressed her son, whose cheeks were beginning to color. He seemed to be protesting what his mother had just told him or commanded him to do.

More than ever Hansard was distressed by the vast silence of his present world. It may be amusing for a few moments to watch television with the sound cut off, but it is quite another thing when you see the words spilling soundlessly from your own son's lips.

The man in the black hair-bubble concluded what

58

must have been an argument by pushing Nathan Junior gently but firmly into the outer hall and locking the door behind him. Hansard followed his son into the elevator. He knew from experience that no elevator in S-S Manors could move quickly enough to be any danger to him.

S-S Manors had been so designed that children played on the high rooftops instead of cluttering up the sidewalks and streets below. The architects had designed the lofty playgrounds with considerable imagination and poor materials, and now the labyrinth, the honeycomb of playhouses, and the elaborate jungle-gym were all in the first stages of disintegration. Originally a cyclone fence had screened the entire play area, but there were only a few shreds and tatters left. Even the guardrails were broken through in places.

As soon as Nathan Junior came out of the elevator he was herded into the labyrinth by an older boy. Hansard followed him inside. The twisting concrete corridors were jammed with children, all as small or smaller than his son. Any kind of games were out of the question here. The rest of the playground was monopolized by the older boys for their own games.

Nathan Junior fought his way to a group of his own friends. They stood together whispering, then the seven of them ran pell-mell out of the labyrinth toward that corner of the roof where a game of isometric baseball was in progress. The leader of the escapees (not Nathan Junior) caught the ball and ran with it back to the labyrinth. Nathan Junior, not being a very good runner, lagged behind and was caught by one of the older boys.

This boy—he was about fourteen—took hold of Nathan Junior by the ankles, turned him upside down, and carried him to the edge of the roof where the fencing had been caved through. He held the smaller boy, twisting and screaming (though for Hansard it happened in dumbshow), out over the abyss. It was a sheer drop of thirty-five stories to the street. He let go of one ankle. Hansard had to turn away. He told himself that what he was seeing was a common occurrence, that it had probably happened

59

to every one of the children up here at one time or another, that his son was in no real danger. It helped not at all.

At last the torture was brought to an end, and Nathan Junior was allowed to return to the little prison that the architects had unwittingly provided. *I'll leave now,* Hansard told himself. *I should never have come here.* But he was no more able to follow his own good advice than he had been to help his son. He followed him into the labyrinth once more.

Nathan Junior pushed his way through to where his friends were, and immediately he struck up an argument with a slightly younger and smaller boy. The victim became the aggressor. A fight started, and it was clear that the smaller boy stood no chance against Nathan Junior, who was soon sitting on his chest and pounding his head against the concrete surface of the roof.

"Stop it!" Hansard yelled at his son. "For God's sake, stop it!"

But Nathan Junior, of course, could not hear him.

Hansard ran out of the labyrinth and down the thirty-four flights of stairs to the street. In his haste he would sometimes plunge through walls or trample over the residents of the building who used the stairwells as their community center, *faute de mieux.* But at street level he had to rest. He had not eaten for five days. He was very weak. Without having intended to, he fell into a light slumber.

And he was there again, in the country that was so intensely green. But now it was black, and a buzzing was in his ears. It was black, and the flame thrower was in his hands, his own hands. The little boy who had broken out from the stockade—he could not have been more than four years old—was running across the blackened field toward him. Such a small boy, such a very small boy: how could he run carrying that heavy carbine? His arms were too short for him to raise it to his shoulder, so that when he fired it he had to let the devastated earth itself receive the recoil. He ran forward screaming his hatred, but for some reason Hansard could hear nothing but the buzzing of the flame thrower. He ran forward, such a very small

60

boy, and when he was close enough Hansard let him have it with the flame thrower.

But the face that caught fire was no longer a little chink face. *It was Nathan Junior's.*

When Hansard, considerably weakened by his exertions of the afternoon, returned to the reservoir that night to drink and fill his canteen, he found that the high barrier that had been built around the pumping station was being patrolled by Worsaw's men. Throughout the night the men kept doggedly to their posts. From a distance Hansard reconnoitered their position and found no flaw in it. The lamps of the Real World shone brightly on the streets surrounding the barrier, and there was no angle from which Hansard might approach near enough unseen to the barrier to be able to swim the rest of the way underground.

At dawn the men surrendered their posts to a second shift. *They must be running out of meat,* Hansard thought. His canteen had given out. He had very little strength left. In a siege he had no doubt that they would outlast him.

And therefore, he decided, *I shall have to make my raid tonight.*

He returned to the library stacks to sleep, not daring to go to sleep within hearing range of his hunters, for it was only too likely that he would wake up screaming. He usually did now.

SEVEN

SCIAMACHY

Since there was a danger that he might exhaust all his strength in rehearsals, after the second trial run he rested on the library steps and basked in the warm air of late April. He could not, so weak as this, so hungry as this, take much satisfaction in mere warmth and quiet—unless it could be called a satisfaction to drift off into cloudy, unthinking distances. The sun swooped down from noonday to the horizon in seeming minutes. The simulated stars of the dome winked on, winked off.

Now.

He walked over to the Gove Street intersection. Half a mile further down, Gove Street ran past the pumping station. A number of cars were stopped at the intersection for a red light. Hansard got into the back seat of a taxi beside a young lady in a mink suit. The taxi did not start off with too sudden a jerk, and Hansard was able to stay on the seat.

The pumping station came in sight. The taxi would pass by it, many feet nearer than Hansard would have been able to approach by himself. He took a deep breath and tensed his body. As soon as the taxi was driving parallel with the barrier Hansard leaped through the floor and down into the roadway. He could only hope that he had vanished into the pavement before either of the men guarding this face of the barrier had had a chance to notice him.

He had rehearsed the dive, but not the swimming. Earlier, he had discovered that without the onus of necessity he possessed neither the strength nor the breath for sustained effort. This was not a clear guarantee that, given the necessity, he *would* find the strength. (It is all very well to praise the heroic virtues, but strength is finally a simple matter of carbohydrates and proteins.) It was a chance he had to take.

A foolish chance—for already he could feel his strength failing, his arms refusing another stroke, his lungs demanding air, taking control of his protesting will; his arms reaching up, to the air; his body breaking through the surface, into the air; his lungs, the air, ah, ah yes!

And it was not after all a failure—not yet, for he had come up seven feet on the other side of the barrier. Seven feet! He would have been surprised to find he'd swum that far altogether.

Ives had said there were at least seventeen men, and probably more. Two men guarded each of the four faces of the barrier and they worked in two shifts. That would account for sixteen. And the seventeenth—wouldn't he be guarding the reservoir itself?

He would be.

And he would be Worsaw.

Reasoning thus, Hansard decided, in spite of his weariness, to swim up the hill. It wasn't necessary to go the whole distance in a single effort. He stripped for easier swimming, hung the .45 he had taken from Ives's pack in a sling fixed to his belt. Then, inchmeal, keeping as much as possible within the interstices of flowerbeds and shrubs he advanced up the slope. He could see guards about the station, but they seemed to be guards of the Real World.

Swimming, he thought of water, of the dryness in his throat, of water, the water filling the immaterial shell of the pumping station. He had, since his first visit here, developed a theory to account for what he had seen then. The ghostly water produced by the echo-effect of transmission was contained by the floor and walls of the station, just as the ground of the Real World supported the ghostly Hansard. The *why* of this was as yet obscure to him, but he was pragmatist enough to content himself with the *how* of most things.

When the pressure of the mounting water became too great the excess quantity of it simply sank through the floor of the station. Just so, Hansard could submerge himself in the ground by entering it with sufficient force. As for the turbulent bubbling he had observed, that was undoubtedly caused by the "echo" of the air that the other pump was producing as it transmitted air to the Mars Command Posts. The air pump was below the level attained by the water, and so the ghostly air would be constantly bubbling up through the ghostly water and escaping through the skylight in the ceiling.

About thirty feet from the station Hansard was confronted with a blank stretch of lawn from which the nearest cover, a plot of tulips, was eight feet distant. Hansard decided to swim for it underground.

He came up on the wrong side of the flowerbed and was blinded at once by the beam of a flashlight. He ducked back into the ethereal subsurface with Worsaw's rebel yell still ringing in his ears. Below the surface he could hear nothing, though he deduced, from the sudden stinging sensation in his left shoulder, that Worsaw was firing at him.

Without knowing it was stupid or cunning, only because he was desperate and had no better plan (though none worse either), Hansard swam straight toward his enemy, toward where he supposed him still to be. He surfaced only a few feet away.

Swearing, Worsaw threw his emptied pistol at the head that had just bobbed up out of the lawn.

Hansard had taken out his .45, but before he could use it he had to fend off Worsaw's kick. The man's heavy combat boot grazed Hansard's brow and struck full force against the hand that held the automatic. The weapon flew out of his hand.

Hansard had drawn himself halfway out of the ground, but before he could get to his feet Worsaw had thrown himself on top of him, grabbing hold of Hansard's shoulders and pressing them back into the earth. Hansard tried to pull Worsaw's hands away, but he was at a disadvantage—and he was weak.

Slowly Worsaw forced Hansard's face below the surface of the earth and into the airless, opaque ether below. Hansard grappled with the other man, not in an effort to resist him—he had too little strength for that—but to guarantee that when he went under Worsaw would go under with him. So long as they maintained the struggle there was no force to prevent their sinking thus, together, into the earth; eyes open but unseeing, going down ineluctably, neither weakening yet, though surely the first to weaken would be Hansard. And then?

And then, curiously, the chill turpentine-like substance of the earth seemed to give way to another substance. Hansard could feel the water—real and tangible—fill his nostrils and the hollows of his ears. The water within the building, seeping through the floor under its own pressure, had spread out to form a sort of fan-shaped water table beneath the station. It was to the edge of this water table that the two men had descended in their struggle.

Worsaw's grip loosened—he did not assimilate novelty so quickly—and Hansard was able to break away from him. He swam now into the water table and upward, and in a short time he was within the transmitting station, though still under water. He surfaced and caught his breath. If only Worsaw did not realize too quickly where . . .

But already Worsaw, deducing where Hansard had gone, had entered the transmitting station and was swimming up after him—like the relentless monster of a nightmare that pursues the dreamer through any landscape that is conjured up, which, even when it has once been killed, rises up again to continue the pursuit.

Hansard took a deep breath and dove down to confront the nightmare. He caught hold of Worsaw's throat, but his grip was weak and Worsaw tore his hands away. Improbably, he was smiling, and his red hair and beard waved dreamily in the clear water. Worsaw's knee came up hard against Hansard's diaphragm, and he felt the breath go out of his lungs.

Then Hansard was unable to see any more. His upper body was once more plunged into "solid" matter. Surely they had not already sunk as far as the floor in their struggle?

Suddenly Worsaw released his grip. Hansard fought free and surfaced. The water was tinged a deep pink. Had his shoulder wound bled that much?

The headless corpse of ex-Sergeant Worsaw floated up lazily to the surface, air still bubbling out the windpipe.

Hansard did not at once understand. Their fight had carried them into the transmitter itself. It was then that Hansard had found himself unable to see. Worsaw, unthinkingly pursuing his advantage, had entered the transmitter at a point several inches above Hansard's point of entry, and passed through the plane of transmission. The various molecules of his head had joined the stream of water that was being transmitted continuously to Mars.

Finding an area of water as yet untainted by the blood,

Hansard drank, then filled his canteen. He dragged the decapitated body down through the water and outside the station. There he shoved it beneath a tulip bed. It was a better burial than he would have received at Worsaw's hands.

He checked the wound in his shoulder. It was superficial.

It seemed strange, now that he thought of it, that Worsaw's confederates had not come in response to the shots that had been fired; more than strange. He looked about desperately for the lost .45.

Then Hansard heard it.

It sounded like a marching band advancing down Gove Street. From the prominence of the hill Hansard could see much of Gove Street, and it was filled with nothing but its usual swift stream of headlights. The invisible marching band became very loud. It was playing *The Stars and Stripes Forever*.

EIGHT

BRIDGETTA

The same afternoon that Hansard had waited out, drowsy, hungry, half aware, on the steps of the Arlington Library witnessed elsewhere a dialogue that was to be of decisive consequence for our story. Herewith a small part of that conversation:

"*We* are all in agreement."

"But when aren't you, popsicle? *We're* in agreement too, you know."

"If it's a question of food, then one of us is perfectly willing to go without. We're already overpopulated, or we will be by tomorrow. Besides, I should think you'd *enjoy* a new face around here."

"It is not a matter of largesse, and you are mistaken to think that I could prefer any face to your own. Your cheeks are like pomegranates, your nose like a cherry. You are another Tuesday Weld."

"For heaven's sake, Tuesday Weld is pushing *fifty,* grandfather!"

"Grandfather, indeed! I'm your husband. Sometimes I think you don't believe it. Is that why you want that young stud around here, so you can be unfaithful to me? Frailty, thy name is—"

"I should like to have the *opportunity.* What good is virtue that is never tried?"

"I am deeply hurt." Then, after a suitable pause: "But it is so typically American a name, like Coca-Cola on the tongue: Tuesday Weld."

"The Army's also typically American. But you won't give him a chance."

"*You* will, I'm sure, my darling. Is it his uniform you love him for?"

"He cuts a handsome figure in his uniform. I can't deny it."

"Oof! I hate uniforms. I hate people from the Army. They want to destroy the world. They are *going* to destroy the world. And they would like to keep me prisoner forever—God damn the Army. There is no justice. I am outraged."

She, calmly: "But if they're going to destroy the world it seems all the better reason why, while there's still time, we might show some charity."

"All right, then, you can have his head on a silver platter. I knew from the first you wouldn't stop till you'd had your way. If you can find him before *they* do, you can bring him home and feed him a meal. Like a stray dog, eh? But if he makes messes, or whines at night . . ."

"We get rid of him, my love. Of course."

"Kiss me, popsicle. No, not there—on the nose."

Hansard walked down the slope to where he had left his clothes. He dressed, hesitated, then walked through the wall built about the power station. Worsaw's confederates had disappeared. A very few late strollers passed by on the sidewalk; taxis and buses sped past in the street; and all these soundless goings-on were accompanied by the incongruous Sousa march-tune, as though a film were being shown with the wrong sound track.

He was very weak. Indeed if it had not been for this supererogatory strangeness, he would very likely have let himself bed down for the night on the roof of the power station.

Among the strollers a woman came down the street toward Hansard. Even worn down as he was, even knowing she was of the Real World, and hence inaccessible, he could not help noticing her. In the lamplight her red hair took on a murky tinge of purple. And admirable eyes—what joke made them glint as they did now? The same, doubtless, that curled the corners of her lavender lips. And her figure—what could be inferred of it beneath the jumble of synthetic ostrich plumes of her evening coat—that was admirable too. She reminded him . . .

The woman stopped on the sidewalk, not three feet away from Hansard. She turned to study the blank face of the wall behind Hansard. She seemed, almost, to be looking at *him*.

"I wish she were," he said aloud.

The smile on the woman's thin lips widened. The Sousa march was now very loud, but not too loud to drown the sound of her laughter. It was a discreet laugh, scarcely more than a titter. *But he had heard it.* She lifted a gloved hand and touched the tip of a finger to the end of Hansard's nose. *And he felt it.*

"She *is,* she *is*," the woman said softly. "Or isn't that what you'd wished?"

"I—" Hansard's mouth hung open stupidly. Too many things needed to be said all at once, and the one that took priority was only a banal: "I—I'm hungry."

"And so, perhaps, are those other little men who may still be watching our carcasses for all that John Philip Sousa can do. And therefore I suggest that you follow me, keeping at a healthy distance, until we're well out of the neighborhood. You have strength left in you for another couple miles, I hope."

He nodded his head, and with no more ado she turned on her heel (a low heel, out of keeping with the elegance of the coat) and returned in the direction from which she'd come. Halfway up Gove Street she reached into a window recess and took out a pocket radio and two miniature amplifying units. She turned the radio off, and the music ceased.

"Good thing they were playing Sousa," she commented. "A Brahms quartet wouldn't have been half as frightful. On the other hand a little Moussorgsky . . . And by the way, here's a chocolate bar. That should help for now."

His hand trembled taking off the tinsel wrapping. The taste of the chocolate exploded through his mouth like a bomb, and tears welled from his eyes. "Thank you," he said, when he had finished eating it.

"I should hope so. But this is still not the place to talk. Follow me a little further. I know a lovely little place on ahead where we can sit down and rest. Are you bleeding? Do you need a bandage? No? Then, come along."

As he followed her this time, the paranoid suspicion came to him that she was fattening him up on chocolate bars, as the witch fattened Hansel, so that when it was time to cook him he would make a better meal. It did not occur to him, then, that if she had a source of chocolate bars she wouldn't have to cook *him*. But he was very weak and most of his attention had to be devoted, lightheaded as he was, to the business of staying upright.

After a few turnings and short-cuts through opaque obstacles she led him up the steps of a brightly-lighted Howard Johnson's. They sat across from each other in a green-and-orange plastic booth, where she presented him with a second candy bar and accepted his offer of a drink from the canteen.

"I suppose I should introduce myself," she said.

"I'm sorry. I seem to remember your face from somewhere, but I can't remember . . ."

"*But*—I was about to say—I *won't* introduce myself, not quite yet at least. Not until you've told me something about yourself."

With marvelous restraint Hansard pushed the remaining half of the candy bar aside. "My name is Nathan Hansard. I'm a captain in the United States Army, serial number—"

"Oh, for heaven's sake, this isn't a prisoner-of-war camp. Just tell me what's happened to you since you went through the manmitter."

When Hansard had finished his narrative, she nodded her head approvingly, making the high-piled hair (which was a much healthier shade of red under the incandescent light) to tremble becomingly. "Very noble, Captain. Really very noble and brave, as you realize full-well without *my* saying so. I see now I was wrong not to have spoken to you yesterday."

"Yesterday? Ah, now I do remember. You were looking at me from the other side of the reflecting pool."

She nodded, and went on: "But you can understand why we've had to be suspicious. Just because a man is good-looking is no guarantee he won't want to . . . put me in his cooking pot."

Hansard smiled. Fortified by the candy bars, he was able to concentrate more of his attention on the personal graces of his benefactress. "I understand. In fact I have to confess that I wasn't without suspicions of my own when I was following you up Gove Street a little while ago. You look so . . . well-fed."

"Ah, you have a smooth tongue, Captain. You'll surely turn my head with your flattery. Another candy bar?"

"Not just now, thank you. And I must also thank you, I think, for saving my life. It was your radio, wasn't it, that turned them away?"

"Yes. I had been waiting farther up Gove Street, hoping I could spot you before they did. I didn't know where else to look, but I was certain the transmitter would be your only source of water. But you got through the wall without my ever seeing you. When I heard the gunshots I had to assume you were already inside, and I turned on the radio full blast. Once one has become accustomed to the silences of this world, music takes on a rather dreadful intensity. Or rather, I suppose, we're able to hear it the way it was meant to be heard."

"Well, again I must thank you. Thank you, Miss . . . ?"

"Mrs."

"Excuse me. With your gloves on, I couldn't tell."

70

"But you can just call me Bridgetta. My husband calls me Jet, but I think that's vulgar. Of course, so does he—that's why he uses it. He thinks it's American to be vulgar. He doesn't understand that vulgarity isn't fashionable any more. It's because he first arrived in the States in the late Sixties that—"

"I'm afraid . . . I'm afraid you'll have to speak a bit more slowly. My mind isn't as quick as it would be if it had a full stomach."

"Excuse me. Panofsky."

"Panofsky?" He was more than ever lost.

"You asked my name, and that's what it is—Mrs. Panofsky, Bridgetta Panofsky, wife of Bernard. You've perhaps heard of my husband?"

"God damn," Hansard said. *"God damn!"*

There were many celebrities of that year—writers, actors, or criminals—who might have entertained as high an estimate of their own notoriety and of whom Hansard would have been as unaware as we today perforce must be. But the name Panofsky was known to everyone. Literally, to *all*. "I've heard of him, yes," Hansard said.

Bridgetta smiled coolly, allowing him time to reassemble his composure.

"Then that's why—" Hansard exclaimed, as he began to program himself with remembered data.

"Yes," she said, "that's why we're like you—*sublimated.*"

"Eh? I'm afraid I never had time to read Freud."

"Sublimated is only Bernie's word for being *this* way." Illustratively, she brushed her hand through a bouquet of plastic flowers that graced the Formica tabletop. "You see, the powers-that-be have let Bernie equip the homestead with transmitters so he can carry on his research there. Bernie can do just about anything, if he tells them it's for research. Except drive out the front door. The existence of the transmitters in Elba—that's what we call the homestead—is strictly . . . what's the favorite word now for very, *very* private?"

"Priority-A."

"Just so. And for once the whole rigmarole has worked

71

to his advantage. Since no one knows we have transmitters, no one comes to bother us at Elba—as they do in the State Department."

"The State Department! I saw you there too—almost a week ago. I'm sure it was you, except your hair was another color. And the man with you, in the wheelchair, that would have been Panofsky?"

"Panofsky-Sub-One, if you saw him in the State Department."

"Again, slowly?"

"We use a numeral subscript to distinguish between our different levels of reality. For instance, there must be a Nathan Hansard on Mars now. He'd be Hansard-Sub-One, and you're Hansard-Sub-Two."

"But if you know the State Department manmitter is watched, why do you use it?"

"We only use it coming back from someplace, not going there. A week ago—where would we have been coming from? Moscow, I think. Borominska was premiering in a revival of Tudor's *Lilac Garden*. Bernie insisted on being there."

Hansard recalled now, from a long-ago article in *Time*, the fact that Panofsky was an ardent balletomane and made frequent—and instantaneous—excursions via manmitter to the world's ballet capitals throughout their seasons, these brief tours being the single concession that the government had agreed to make to Panofsky for the loss of his freedom. At any performance of significance Panofsky was to be seen in the box of honor, or, at the intermission, outside his box, presiding regally over a strange mélange of secret service guards and ballet enthusiasts, always the dominating figure in such groups —even in his wheelchair.

"Tell me," she asked after a pause, "do you like me better as a redhead?"

"It's hard to decide. There's something to be said on both sides of the question."

She cocked her head slyly and smiled. "Say, Captain Hansard, I'm glad you're here."

"The feeling is mutual, Mrs. Panofsky. I'd rather be having a steak dinner with you than with "A" Company."

"We'll have some fun together, Captain."

"But some food first?"

"Mmm." Bridgetta Panofsky leaned forward through Howard Johnson's Formica tabletop and, apropos of nothing, she laid a gloved hand on Nathan Hansard's throat and slowly, deliberately, and a little insistently kissed his lips.

"Hey, you're married, remember?"

Her laughter was too self-assured to be due to embarrassment. "Such an old-fashioned *pickle*," she commented, as she stood to leave. "But I rather like that."

Jesus Christ, Hansard thought to himself. He thought it with such force that he wasn't quite sure he had not said it aloud. For Hansard's moral sense was too finely formed to tolerate a double standard. The notion of adultery with another man's wife was as noxious to him as, years before, his own wife's adultery had been. In any case, moral sense notwithstanding, he had scarcely had an opportunity yet to be tempted; nor was he, given that opportunity, in condition to respond to it.

Perhaps this was what she had in mind when Bridgetta said to him, as they left the restaurant, "First thing, we'll get some chicken broth into your belly, and then maybe some soft-boiled eggs. But no steaks—not for a day or so. Do you like curries? Bernie makes very good curries."

"Don't know. Never had curry."

"Lord, you *are* a military man! I've always liked men in uniform, but Bernie doesn't feel that way at all. Oh, now you've started blushing again. Really, you don't have the blood to waste on blushing, Captain."

"You'll have to excuse me," Hansard said stiffly.

"No, no," Bridgetta said, with an abrupt shift of mood, "you'll have to excuse *me*. You see, if the truth be told, Captain, if you could see what I'm feeling tonight, you'd see . . ." She broke off for a while, then continued, shaking her head as though in anger for her own awkwardness. "I'm afraid, that's all. And when a person is afraid—why,

73

then she reaches out. You know? Will you hold my hand at least? Like that. Thank you."

After they had walked on a way he asked, "What are you afraid of?"

"Why, what is anybody afraid of, Captain?"

"I don't know."

"Of dying, certainly."

NINE

PANOFSKY

"You'll have to admit," Bridie said, "that he's smart."

"Smart, smart, what is smart?" asked Panofsky. "A rat that runs a maze is smart. I'm smart. President Madigan is smart."

"And that he's polite and respectful," Jet added.

"At the moment, that is only a part of being smart," snapped the other Panofsky. "You might as well say that because he's good-looking—"

"He does have an honest face," said Bridget firmly.

"Because he doesn't often smile," said the first Panofsky.

"He was humorous enough with *me*, love," Jet argued. "You forget at times how much you throw most people off balance. Captain Hansard didn't know what to make of you last night."

"Goulash or shishkebab, eh?"

"That's being perfectly unfair," Bridget objected in her loftiest tone. "You heard everything the good captain said at Howard Johnson's over Jet's little transmitter. Not only is he not a *cannibal*, he's also the last of the Puritans—by the looks of it." The other two Bridgettas nodded their heads in glum confirmation.

"But there's no need to write him off *yet*," Jet said, rallying. "He just needs to get his strength back."

"I think you're missing Bridget's point," Bridie said. "In her gentle way she was suggesting that you went after

74

him too quickly. Why, the poor man must suppose that he's escaped from a den of cannibals into a nest of vampires."

"Girls, girls," said both Panofskys together. Then the one who wore the knitted skull cap (possession of which gave its wearer priority at such times) continued: "I have no desire to engage in a debate on the merits of different strategies of seduction. I only wish to counsel you not to set your hearts too much on keeping him. Remember, he is in the Army; and while you're admiring the uniform, watch out for the iron heel. Perhaps Bridie is right about going slow with him. He's survived this long only by having a too-rigid character. If it cracks there's no telling what will come out from the old shell. But I'm certain I'd rather not find out. Do you agree with me, Bernard?"

"Entirely, Bernard."

"Then to your posts—and may the best woman win."

"Did you sleep well, Captain?"

"Very well, thank you." Hansard sat up from the mattress on which he had spent the night. "How do you do it?"

"The mattress, you mean? Bernie has to take all the credit for provisioning us. In fact, you have Bernie to thank for this too. It's his breakfast, but he thought you'd appreciate it more."

Bridget held out the tray she was carrying. It held a plate of three fried eggs, other plates of bacon and toast, a pint glass of orange juice, a silver scallop-dish of jam, and an antique coffee server from the Plaza Hotel. Steam rose from the spout of the server.

"After you've eaten I'll have some water ready for you to shave with, unless you'd rather let your beard grow out."

"Amazing," said Hansard, oblivious for the first few moments of anything but the breakfast. After one egg, however, he looked up. "You're a different color today," he observed. For *this* Bridgetta's hair was not red but

75

flaxen-blond and braided into a tight crown about her head, Irish-peasant-style.

"I'm a different girl altogether. It was Jet who rescued you yesterday. She's the beauty of the family. I'm Bridget —I take care of household things. And you've still to meet Bridie, the intellectual one."

"But aren't you all the same person? I mean, you speak as though the others were your older sisters."

"In a sense they are. It's important, if only for our self-concept, that we should be able to tell each other apart. So we try, by division of labor, to split the old single Bridgetta-identity into three. The youngest always has to be Bridget, because obviously that's the least fun."

"The youngest?"

"The one to have come out of the manmitter most recently is the youngest. You understand how it works, don't you? It's sort of like an echo. Well, the echo that's me has only been here a week. Jet, who was Bridget before I came, has been here four months now. And Bridie has been around from the very start, two years ago. You can always tell which of us is which because I'm blond and wear an apron; Jet is a redhead and dresses alamode, and Bridie is a sort of ashy brunette and has a moldy old lab coat. It's remarkable how easily clothes can dictate one's behavior."

"And your husband, are there more than one of him?"

"Two. But we thought we'd only confront you with one of each of us last night to keep things simple. Bernard is always just Bernard. He doesn't bother to differentiate between his two selves the way we do. In any case, there's very little that could threaten *his* self-concept. Tell me, Captain, do you like me better as a blonde or as a redhead?"

Hansard shook his head, as though to clear away cobwebs. "For a moment there you really did have me believing you were a different person than the girl I met last night, but when you said that I knew better."

"Excuse me, Captain, it's not always easy to remember to keep in character as a drudge. Even Cinderella has moments, when her sisters are away. . . . You ate all that so fast! Do you want more?"

"Not now."

"Then, if you please, come with me. Bernard wants to have a word with you." It was like following a teacher to the principal's office. Hansard wondered what he could possibly have done wrong already.

"I can't tell you how much I appreciate your hospitality, Doctor Pan—"

"Then don't make the attempt, Mr. Hansard. You will excuse me if I do not employ your proper title, but for me it would be a pejorative form. My experiences with the American military, and before that with the military establishments of East Germany and the Third Reich, have been, on the whole, unhappy experiences. You may use the same informality in addressing me. In America I have always felt that that 'Doctor' of yours also has a pejorative sense when it refers to someone outside the medical profession. Dr. Strangelove, for instance, or Dr. Frankenstein."

"I'll try and remember that, sir. I certainly didn't intend any disrespect."

"How old are you, Mr. Hansard?"

"Thirty-eight."

"Married?"

"Divorced."

"So much the better. You are just the right age for my Bridgetta. She is twenty-seven."

"Just the right age for your Bridgetta for *what*, sir?"

"For what!" The two Panofskys laughed in chorus. Then, pointing at his double, the Panofsky wearing the skull cap said: "Do you not see those wispy gray hairs? That shrunken chest? Do you not realize that that old man is paralyzed from the waist down?"

"Nonsense, Bernard!" said the double.

"Please to remember, Bernard," said Panofsky, laying his hand on the skull cap, "that I have the floor. And allow me a little poetic license in stating my case. Where was I? From the waist down, yes. Do you not see me

77

here before you in a wheel chair? And you ask *'For what?'*
Are you naïve, my good Captain?"

"It's not that exactly," Hansard mumbled, shifting his
gaze uneasily from one Panofsky to the other.

"Or, perhaps, though you're willing enough to go out
and kill people or to push the button that will destroy
the world, you have too fine a moral sense to think of a
little hanky-panky?"

"It may surprise you to learn that some of us military
men *do* have a moral sense—*Doctor*."

"Ah, he's got you there, Bernard," said the Panofsky
without the cap. "Dead to rights."

"If you have an objection, Mr. Hansard, please to state
it."

"Much as I admire your wife's fine qualities—"

"My wives, rather. There are presently three women
meriting the distinction."

"Lovely as all three are, they are *your* wives, sir. And
I don't believe in, uh, promiscuity. Not with another man's
wedded wife."

"Really, Captain?" Both old gentlemen leaned forward
in their wheel chairs. "Excuse me, but is that your *sincere* objection?"

"I might have others, but I wouldn't know of them
yet. The one I stated is sufficient in itself to be a basis
for decision. Why should you question my sincerity?"

"Ask him if he's a Catholic, Bernard," said the Panofsky without the cap.

"Bernard, if you want to take over this discussion, I
will give you my cap. As it happens I was about to ask
him just that question. Well, Captain?"

"No, sir. I was raised a Methodist, but it's been a few
years since I've been in any kind of church at all."

Both Panofskys sighed. "The reason we asked," the
first explained, "is that it's so unusual today to find a
young man of your convictions. Even within the church.
We are both Catholics, you see, though that becomes a
problematical statement at the present time. Are we in
fact *two*? But that's all theology, and I won't go into that
now. As for these scruples of yours, I think they can be

78

cleared up easily. You see, our marriage is of a rather fictitious quality. Bridgetta is my wife in—what is that nice euphemism, Bernard?"

"In name only."

"Ah, yes! My wife in name only. Further, we were wed in a civil ceremony instead of before a priest. We married each other with the clear understanding that there were to be no children. Even had we had such an intention it is highly doubtful, considering my age, that it could have been accomplished. In the eyes of Holy Mother Church such a marriage is no marriage at all. If we had access to the machinery of canon law an annulment could be obtained with ease. But after all, an annulment is only a formality, a statement that says that what does not exist has never happened.

"Consider, if you prefer, that Bridgetta is my daughter rather than my wife. That is more usual in these cases, isn't it—that the wise old scientist, or the evil old scientist, as the case may be, should have a lovely daughter to give to the hero? And I've never heard it to happen that the hero refuses her."

"What was the point in having married her at all, if what you say is so?"

"My civil marriage to Bridgetta, whom, you must understand, I dearly love, is a *mariage de convenance*. I need an heir, someone who can inherit from me; for I have earned, from the government and through patent contracts, a fantabulous amount of money—"

"Fantabulous—how vulgar!" observed the double quietly.

"Yes, but how *American*! And so I married Bridgetta, who had been my laboratory assistant, so that she might inherit from me. Otherwise it would go to the government, for whom I have no great love. Then, too, someone must carry on my legal battles in the courts after I'm dead—"

"Against the Emergency Allocations Act, you know."

"*I'm* telling this, Bernard. And finally I need someone to talk to in this gloomy prison besides the secret service guards and brainwashed lab technicians they assign to me. I'm not allowed to hold private conversations with my colleagues from the university any more, because they're afraid I'll leak their secret weapon . . . which *I* invented! In just such a manner as this was Prometheus dealt with for giving man the gift of fire."

"Now, Bernard, don't overexcite yourself. Better give me the cap for a while now, and I'll straighten out matters with the captain. I think we can come to an understanding that will satisfy everyone—"

But before this happy accord could be reached they were interrupted by Bridgetta—a fourth version, with black hair—who entered through the door at the farther end of the room. Bridget, Jet, and Bridie followed closely after.

"She's going through," Bridie announced. And indeed it was so, for the new, black-haired Bridgetta walked on relentlessly toward and then through her husband, who seemed not at all perplexed by the experience.

"That was Bridgetta-Sub-One, of course," his double explained to Hansard. "Otherwise, you know, she wouldn't go around the house opening doors instead of, like any proper ghost, walking through them. Bridgetta Sub-One is leaving for Paris. *Candide* is at the Opéra Comique. It was in expectation of her departure that I wanted to speak to you down *here* instead of in my usual rooms upstairs, for that—on the other side of the second door Bridgetta opened—that is our manmitter-in-residence."

Bridgetta-Sub-One closed the door of what had seemed, to Hansard, no more than a closet behind her. The six people watched the closed door in perfect, unbreathing silence, and in a moment a hand appeared through the oak panel. One could sense in the startled gestures of that hand all the wonderment that must have been on the woman's face. Panofsky purred forward in his chair and lifted his own hand up to catch hold of hers, and how much relief and happiness there was in the answering clasp of her hand.

Now the woman who had lately been Bridgetta-Sub-One stepped through the door, smiling but with her eyes tight shut, an inescapable reaction to walking through one's first door.

She opened her eyes. "Why, then, it's true! You were right, Bernie!"

The two Panofskys chuckled indulgently, as though to say, "Aren't I always right?" but forbore to be more explicit. It was her birthday party, not his.

The new Bridgetta-Sub-Two regarded her three doubles with an amused and slightly fearful smile, then, for the first time, lifted her eyes to see the figure standing behind them. The smile disappeared, or if it did not quite disappear, it changed into a much more serious kind of smile.

"Who is he?" she whispered.

Hansard wasn't able to answer, and no one else seemed about to rescue him from his difficulty. Hansard and Bridgetta stood regarding each other in silence, smiling and not quite smiling, for a long time.

In the following days it became a matter of dispute between them (but the very gentlest of disputes) whether what had happened could be legitimately said to be, at least in Hansard's case, love at first sight.

After the curry dinner that Panofsky had prepared to welcome the new Bridgetta, after the last magnum of champagne had been emptied and the glasses tossed out through the closed windows, the two Panofskys took Hansard into a spacious library in one corner of which a third Panofsky (Sub-One) was leafing through a handsome folio volume of neo-Mondrian equations.

"Oh, don't mind *him*," Panofsky reassured Hansard. "He's really the easiest person in the world to live with. We ignore him, and he ignores us. I took you aside so that we might continue our discussion of this afternoon. You see, Mr. Hansard—may I call you Nathan?—we are living here under most precarious circumstances. Despite our sometimes luxuriousness, we have no resources but those which the Panofsky and Bridgetta of the Real World —a nice phrase that, Nathan, I shall adopt it, with your permission, for my own—can think to send us.

"We have a certain store of canned foods and smoked ham and such set aside for emergencies, but that is not a firm basis for faith in the future, is it? Have you much considered the future? Have you wondered what you'll do a year from now? Ten years? Because, as the book says, you can't go home again. The process by which we came into being *here* is as irreversible as entropy. In fact, in the largest sense, it is only another manifestation of the Second Law. In short, we're stuck here, Nathan."

"I suppose, in a case like that, sir, it's best not to think too much about the future. Just try and get along from day to day."

"Good concentration-camp philosophy, Nathan. Yes, we must try and endure. But I think, at the same time, you must admit that certain of the old rules of the game don't apply. You're *not* in the Army now."

"If you mean that matter about my scruples, sir, I've thought of a way my objection might be overcome. As a captain I have authority to perform marriages in some circumstances. It seems to me that I should have the authority to grant a divorce as well."

"A pity you had to go into the Army, Nathan. The Jesuits could have used a casuist like you."

"However, I must point out now that a divorce is no guarantee that a romance follows immediately after, though it may."

"You mean you'd like me to leave off matchmaking? You Americans always resent that kind of assistance, don't you? Very well, you're on your own, Nathan. Now, hop to it."

"And I also want it understood that I'm not promiscuous. Those four women out there may all have been one woman at one time, but now there are *four* of them. And only one of me."

"Your dilemma puts me in mind of a delightful story of Boccaccio's. However, I shall let you settle that matter with the lady, or ladies themselves."

At that moment three of the ladies in question entered the room. "We thought you'd want to know, Bernie," said Jet, "that Bridget is dead."

82

"What!" said Hansard.

"Nothing to become excited about, Nathan," Panofsky said soothingly. "These things have to happen."

"She committed suicide, you see," the new Bridgetta explained to Hansard, who had not seemed to be much comforted by Panofsky's bland assurance.

"But *why*?" he asked.

"It's all in Malthus," said Bridie. "A limited food supply; an expanding population—something's got to give."

"You mean that whenever . . . whenever a new person comes out of the transmitter you just *shoot* somebody?"

"Goodness no!" said Jet. "They take poison and don't feel a thing. We drew lots for it, you see. Everyone but Bridie, because her experience makes her too valuable. Tonight Bridget got the short straw."

"I can't believe you. Don't you value your own life?"

"Of course, but, don't you see?—" Bridgetta laid her hands on the shoulders of her two doubles. "I have more than one life. I can afford to throw away a few as long as I know there's still some of me left."

"It's immoral. It's just as immoral as joining those cannibals."

"Now, Nathan," Panofsky said soothingly, "don't start talking about morality until you know the *facts*. Remember what we said about the old rules of the game? Do you think *I* am an atheist that I would commit suicide just like that, one-two-three? Do you think I would so easily damn my immortal soul? No. But before we can talk about right and wrong we must learn about true and false. I hope you will excuse me from making such expositions, however. I have never enjoyed the simplifications of popular science. Perhaps you would care to instruct the good captain in some first principles, my dear Bridie, and at the same time you could instruct Bridgetta in her new duties."

Bridie bowed her head in a slightly mocking gesture of submission.

"Yes, please," said Hansard. "Explain, explain, explain. From the beginning. In short, easy-to-understand words."

"Well," Bridie began, "it's like this."

TEN

MARS

I should never have joined the Justice-for-Eichmann Committee, he thought. *That was my big mistake. If I hadn't joined the committee I could have been chief-of-staff today.*

But was it, after all, such a terrible loss? Wasn't he happier here? Often as he might denigrate the barren landscape, he could not deny to himself that he gloried in these sharp rock spines, the chiaroscuro, the dust dunes of the crater floors, the bleeding sunsets. *It is all so . . . what? What was the word he wanted?*

It was all so *dead.*

Rock and dust, dust and rocks; the sifted, straining sunlight; the quiet; the strange, doubly-mooned heaven. Days and nights that bore no relation to the days and nights measured off by the earth-synchronized clocks within the station. Consequently there was a feeling of disjunction from the ordinary flow of time, a slight sense of floating, though that might be due to the lower gravity.

Five weeks left. He hoped . . . but he did not name his hope. It was a game he played with himself—to come as near to the idea as he dared and then to scurry away, as a child on the beach scurries away from the frothing ribbons of the mounting tide.

He returned down the olive-drab corridors from the observatory to his office. He unlocked the drawers of his desk and removed a slim volume. He smiled, for if his membership on the ill-fated committee had cost him a promotion, what would happen if it became known that he—Major-General Gamaliel Pittmann—was the American translator of the controversial German poet Kaspar Maas? That the same hand that was now, in a manner of speaking, poised above the doomsday button had also written the famous invocation that opens Maas' *Carbon 14:*

> Let us drop our bombs on Rome
> and cloud the fusing sun,
> at noon, with radium. . . .

Who was it had said that the soul of modern man, Mass Man, was so reduced in size and scope that its dry dust could be wetted only by the greatest art? Spengler? No, somebody after Spengler. All the other emotions were dead, along with God. It was true, at least, of his own soul. It had rotted through like a bad tooth, and he had filled the hollow shell with a little aesthetic silver and lead.

But it wasn't enough. Because the best art—that is, the art to which he found himself most susceptible and which his rotting soul could endorse—brought him only a little closer, and then still a little closer, to the awareness of what it was that underlay the nightingale's sweet tremolos and brought him nearer to naming his unnamed hope.

Fancy cannot cheat so well as she is famed to do.

Yet what else was there? Outside of the silver filling there was only the hollow shell, his life of empty forms and clockwork motions. He was generally supposed to be a happily married man; that is, he had never had the energy to get a divorce. He was the father of three daughters, each of whom had made a good marriage.

Success? Quite a lot of success. And by acting occasionally as a consultant for certain corporations he had so supplemented his Army income that he had no cause to fear for the future. Because he could make agreeable conversation, he moved in the best circles of Washington society.

He was also personally acquainted with President Madigan, and had gone on hunting trips with him in his native Colorado. He had done valuable volunteer work for The Cancer Fund. His article, "The Folly of Appeasement," had appeared in *The Atlantic Monthly* and been commended by no less a personage than former Secretary of State Rusk. His pseudonymous translations of Maas and others of the Munich "Götterdämmerung school" had been widely praised for their finesse, if not always for their content. What else *was* there? He did not know.

He knew, he knew.

He dialed 49 on the phone, the number of Hansard's room. *I'll play a game of Ping-pong,* he thought. Pittmann was an extremely good Ping-pong player. Indeed, he excelled in almost any contest of wits or agility. He was a good horseman, and a passing-fair duelist. In his youth he had represented the United States and the Army in the Olympics Pentathlon.

Hansard was not in his room. Damn Hansard!

Pittmann went back out into the corridor. He looked into the library and game room, but it was empty. For some reason he had grown short of breath.

Darkling, I listen.

Ex-Sergeant Worsaw was outside the door of the control room. He came to attention and saluted smartly. Pittmann paid no attention to him. When he was alone inside the room he had to sit down. His legs trembled, and his chest rose and fell sharply. He let his mouth hang open.

As though of hemlock I had drunk, he thought.

He had never come into the control room like this, never quite so causelessly. Even now, he realized, there was time to turn back.

The control room was unlighted, except for the red ember of the stand-by lamp above the board, which was already set up for Plan B. Pittmann leaned forward and flicked on the television screen. A greatly-magnified color image of the earth, three-quarters dark, appeared.

Love never dies. It is a mistake to suppose that love can die. It only changes. But the pain is still the same.

He looked at the button, set immediately beneath the stand-by light.

Five weeks. Was it possible? Would this be the time? No, no, surely the countermand would come. And yet . . .

Tears welled to Pittmann's gray eyes, and at last he named his hope: "Oh, I want to, I want to. I want to push it *now*."

Hansard had seldom disliked his work so intensely—if it could be called work, for aside from the mock run-throughs of Plan B and the daily barracks inspections, "A" Company had been idle. How are you to keep twenty-five men busy in a small, sealed space that is so fully automated it performs its own maintenance? With isometrics? Pittmann was right: boredom was the great problem on Mars.

Strange, that they didn't rotate the men on shorter schedules. There was no reason they couldn't come here through the manmitter on eight-hour shifts. Apparently the brass who decided such questions were still living in a pretransmitter era in which Mars was fifty million miles away from earth, a distance that one does not, obviously, commute every day.

Hansard had tried to take Pittmann's advice and looked through the library for a long, dull, famous book. He had settled on *Dombey and Son,* though he knew nothing about it and had never before read anything by Dickens. Though he found the cold, proud figure of Dombey somewhat disquieting, Hansard became more and more engrossed with the story. But when, a quarter of the way through the book, Paul Dombey, the "Son" of the title, died, he was unable to continue reading the book. He realized then that it was just that irony in the title, the implied continuity of generations from father to son, that had drawn him to the book. With that promise betrayed, he found himself as bereft as the elder Dombey.

A week had passed, and the order to bomb the nameless enemy had yet to be countermanded. It was too soon to worry, Pittmann had said; yet how could one not worry? Here on Mars, the earth was only the brightest star in the heavens, but that flicker in the void was the home of his wife and son. His ex-wife. Living in Washington, they would surely be among the first to die. Perhaps, for that very reason, they would be among the luckiest. The countermand would certainly be given; there was no need to worry. And yet, what if it were not? Would not Hansard then be, in some small degree, guilty of their deaths, the deaths of Nathan Junior and Marion? Or would he be somehow defending them?

It was of course misleading to consider two lives among the many millions affected. Strategy was global; the policy of optimum benefit was selected by a computer in possession of all the facts.

Guilt? A man may murder another man, or three or four, and be culpable; but who could assume the guilt of megadeaths? Ordinarily the answer would have been simply—the enemy. But the enemy was so far away, and his guilt so ingrained in the confusions of history—camouflaged, so to speak—that sometimes Hansard doubted that the answer was so simple and so convenient for his own conscience.

Unwholesome, purposeless speculations. What had Pittmann said? "Conscience is a luxury for civilians."

Hansard ate his dinner alone, then went to his room and tried to listen to music. But tonight everything sounded like German beer-hall polkas. At last he took a mild barbiturate, standard issue for the men of the Mars Command Posts.

He was walking with Nathan Junior through a field of sere grass. The air was drowsy with the buzzing of flies. They were hunting deer. Nathan Junior carried the shotgun just as his father had shown him to. Hansard carried the lunch pail. Something terrible was going to happen. The color of the grass changed from yellow to brown, from brown to black. There was a loud buzzing in Hansard's ears.

He picked up the receiver of the phone. "Yes?"

"Ah, there you are, Nathan!"

"General Pittmann."

"I thought you might enjoy a game of Ping-pong."

"When?" Hansard asked.

"Right now?"

"That sounds like a good idea," said Hansard. And it did.

ELEVEN

THE NATURE OF THE WORLD

"You have to be very quick," said Bridie, "or it might happen that two objects will occupy the same place at the same time—a highly undesirable condition. That's why we're so careful always to be here from two to three in the afternoon, when transmissions are made."

Hansard snatched away the can of *pâté de foie gras* that the small transmitter had just produced as an echo. The lab technician reached into the right-hand receiver and placed can_1 that he had just transmitted there into the right-hand transmitter. He pressed a button, transmitting can_1 to the left-hand receiver and at the same time producing can_2 which Hansard immediately removed from the transmitter. The pile of $cans_2$ that had been thus produced that afternoon filled a large basket at Hansard's feet.

"It seems to me," said Hansard judiciously, not interrupting his stockpiling, "that all this contradicts the laws of conservation. Where do these cans come from? How does a single can in the Real World produce a gross of cans here?"

"If you want an answer to your question, Nathan, we'll have to start with First Principles. Otherwise it would be like explaining a nuclear reactor to someone who believes in the indivisibility of the atom. In a sense, though, your question isn't far afield from what it was that gave Bernard the whole idea of subspecies of reality. He'd already built the first experimental model of the machine, and the press hadn't decided whether to treat him like God or like a maniac, when he realized that he'd overlooked the notorious fact that every action has an equal and opposite reaction.

"But there seemed to be no reaction corresponding to

.he action of transmission—nothing that could be measured. Of course it *was* there, in the mathematics, and Bernard busied himself with that. Are you familiar with topological transformations? No? But you *do* know that there are non-Euclidean geometries, and that these have the same validity as the common-sense varieties?

"Well, matter transmission is essentially a topological transformation from our world of common-sense spaces to . . . somewhere else, and then back again. It is just at the moment that the transmitted body reaches that 'somewhere else' that the reaction takes place that forms the 'echo.' Which tells you very little, I fear, that you haven't already figured out for yourself. But have patience; I will get to your question.

"The consequence, you see, of Bernard's *ex post facto* reasoning was an entirely new physics, a physics in which our universe is just a special case; indeed, a trivial case, as a point is a trivial case of the circle. There are, in this physics, progressive levels of reality, and matter can exist at each level. Now at the same time that there can be radical changes in the nature of the material world, there need not be corresponding changes in *energic* relationships."

"That is to say?" Hansard asked.

"That is to say that sub-two reality enjoys the same light of common day as sub-one reality, though that light issues from a sun composed of sub-one atoms; a fortunate consequence of the double nature of light, which seems to be both wave and particle—and highly beneficial for us."

"Highly necessary, too. I can see that for myself. But how much energy spillover is there? Sound, for instance, doesn't carry over from the sub-one to the sub-two world."

"Because it is produced by the collision of sub-one particles and carried in a medium of sub-one gases. Similarly we can receive *radiant* heat from the sub-one universe, but not heat produced by conduction or convection. Magnetism and gravity still act on sublimated bodies, but Bernard has proved experimentally that the gravitational attraction isn't mutual. But we'd best not go into that. It's an embarrassing notion for someone like me, who wants to go on living in a comfortable old-fashioned Newtonian universe."

"And you receive radio and television broadcasts from the Real World. I've learned that much."

"Yes, if we possess a sub-two receiver."

"But in that case, why don't you communicate with the Real World by broadcasting to them? Tell them about your situation on short-wave radio."

"Have you ever tried shining a flashlight in the eyes of somebody in the Real World? No? Well, it's the same principle: We can see by *their* sunlight, but they're oblivious to light issuing from a light source constituted of secondary matter. The same would hold true of any radio broadcasts we might make. The Real World always remains real for us secondary creatures—all *too* real. But for primary beings our secondary world might as well not exist, for all the difference it makes to them. No, there is no communication backwards.

"As Bernard pointed out, the sublimation of matter that the transmitter causes is irreversible—another case of entropy, of the universal backsliding of all things. So, no matter how much *pâté* we can pile up *here,* we must permanently remain second-class citizens."

"But in that case I don't understand why Panofsky— Panofsky-Sub-One, that is, back there in the Real World —keeps providing for you."

"Faith," said the new Bridgetta, who was helping Hansard to stack the cans in such a way that they did not become too heavy to keep on top of the floor, "it's all done on faith. We must be thankful that Bernard is a Catholic, and has lots of experience believing unlikely things. Oh, I'm sorry," she said, glancing at Bridie. "It's *your* story."

"You needn't practice being Bridget yet, darling. Not until you've been able to dye your hair. Besides, as it's been two years since I was in the Real World, you're the better qualified to tell about that."

"Once Bernard had figured out the theory behind it," Bridgetta began, "he tried to extrapolate the problems that a sublimated being would have to face in an un-

91

sublimated world. None of the necessities would be available naturally to him: no food, no water, not even air. But he would definitely exist and be alive for as long as one *can* stay alive under such conditions. The first problem was to provide a supply of sublimated air, and fortunately such a supply was at hand in the pumping station that was to be built to supply the Command Posts.

"Bernard invented all kinds of specious reasons for having that transmitter built here under the D.C. Dome instead of, as first planned, by Lake Superior. After only a month of transmitting, the dome would have been filled, and as long as the pumps keep pumping, the supply is more than adequate to compensate for what is lost through the traffic locks. Unfortunately the locations of the general cargo transmitters were specified in the rider to the Emergency Allocation Act, so we couldn't look forward to having all the initial advantages of Robinson Crusoe."

"Though you do have cannibals," Hansard observed.

"That was something else Bernard could do nothing about. He wanted to have the Camp Jackson manmitter built outside the dome, which would have solved our problem neatly."

"And mine too."

"Excuse me, that was a rather careless statement. But he was right: those men do pose a threat. The best we can hope for is that they don't discover us. Fortunately, one doesn't leave footprints here."

"There'd be no problem at all, if you just told the government about this. Then those men could be supplied with the food—and officers—that they need."

"Bernard looks on the government in a different light than you do, Captain," Bridie said rather coldly. "You forget that his relations with the government have not usually been of an agreeable nature. When it has not directly hindered his work, it expropriates and perverts it. No, don't try to argue about that with me, I'm only trying to explain Bernard's attitude. Furthermore, the government's scientists would not have understood the refinements of his theory, for they are still debating the validity of the mathematics on which the transmitter

92

itself was based. Then, if the scientists could be convinced, try to imagine how you would go about explaining to an Army general that there are people just like you and me who are invisible, who can walk through walls and to whom we must send food, though it is probable that we will never, *never* be able to demonstrate—in any tangible way—that they exist."

"When you put it like that, I don't see how he's convinced *himself*."

"Faith," Bridgetta said again, earnestly.

"Faith and reason," Bridie corrected. "Don't forget that Bernard has spent his life as a mathematician. A balanced equation is tangible proof for *him*. Though our existence is abstract at best, he can believe in us just as readily as in the Pythagorean theorem."

"And out of that kernel of belief has come . . . all this?" Hansard waved his hand at the goods lining the shelves of the room. "What possible reason does he give this lab assistant for carrying on this idiot work? It certainly can make no sense to him, if he's unaware that he's producing groceries for us."

"In the case of food, Bernard tells them that he's concerned about possible nutritional losses that might be caused by excessive and repeated transmissions. Preposterous, of course, but you must remember that the very idea of the machine is preposterous to most people. Remember too that the government will do all it can to humor Bernard, so long as he remains tame. The mattress, for instance. Have you heard the story of the mattress?"

Hansard shook his head.

"For a while," Bridgetta said, taking her cue from Bridie, "whenever I was transmitted anywhere, Bernard insisted that I wrap myself in a mattress. To keep myself from being *bumped*, he explained to the secret service guards. Of course, it was really to give *us* something besides a floor to sleep on. But it did make a spectacular entrance at the Paris Embassy. Madame Viandot thought it was a new fashion from New York and ordered three mattresses for herself the next day."

"And no one ever suspects? The things you transmit are so evidently survival items."

"No one has any reason to suspect that survival is a problem for us. The lab assistants, of course, are constantly complaining about the meaningless tasks that Bernard sets for them, and once Bazeley of NASA came around to ask what Bernard was up to. But he only has to hint that he's doing research on a receiverless transmitter, and they fall over themselves to be obliging. For all they know, Bernard's still good for another golden egg."

"Well, does that explain everything, Captain?" Bridie asked.

"Yes, thank you very much. I appreciate your giving me so much time."

Bridie smiled acidly. "But you've forgotten, you know, the biggest problem of all. You haven't learned how it is that you can walk."

"Christ, I've gone all this time without realizing it *was* a problem! How is it that I'm able to walk across the same floor I can swim through?"

"Don't feel dumb, Captain," said Bridgetta. "It's only natural to take for granted that things that you've always been able to do are possible. For Bernard, however, lacking any direct experience, this was the chief theoretical difficulty standing in the way of survival. He could never be certain that as soon as we arrive *here* we just don't start sinking into the ground. That's why *I* was so relieved when I arrived this morning—because I found myself on terra firma. Firm enough, at least, if I don't wear heels."

"But *how* does it work? What keeps me from just sinking down, if gravity is acting on me, as you say?"

"Call it surface tension," said Bridie, "though actually it is a form of potential energy that is inherent in all matter at whatever level of reality. Like static electricity, it forms an equipotential surface over all objects—a sort of 'skin' of energy. What keeps sublimated objects above the ground—the cans on the shelves, for instance, or your feet—is the small repellent force generated by the two surfaces; a force that decreases in proportion to the distance between the two realities.

"Thus a sub-four and, perhaps, a sub-three can *would* sink through a sub-one shelf. But in two adjacent fields of reality the repellent force is quite sufficient for most purposes, though not so great that it cannot be overcome by an opposing force. And therefore second-degree matter can interpenetrate first-degree matter, and you can 'swim' through the floor. All this we've learned here.

"Panofsky-Sub-One has never been able to be sure, and so he keeps providing us with things we really don't need—boards and linoleum rugs. When we try to spread the rugs, they just curl up into the floor. Still, we can be grateful that he errs on the side of caution."

"I am afraid that I *am* sinking deeper and deeper now, though. Sub-three and sub-four cans. I'd never even considered the possibility."

"Imagine what would happen if one of us were transmitted. A sub-two person going through a transmitter would leave behind a sub-three echo of himself. Surely you've been in caves and heard the echo of an echo? As a matter of fact, you've already described such a case. When that unpleasant sergeant donated his head to Mars, the transmission would have produced a sub-three head, though God only knows what's become of it. Sub-one water, as you may have found out, won't support sub-two bodies. A convenient rule-of-thumb is this: After sublimation, the solids of the unsublimated world appear to have the properties of liquids; liquids, the properties of gas, and gas the properties of that unfashionable commodity, an aether."

"But to return a moment to what became of Worsaw-Sub-Two: his head was taken off by a sub-one transmitter. How is that?"

"As I said earlier, energic relationships don't change as one descends the scale of reality. A sub-two transmitter, for instance, could not transmit a sub-one object, but a sub-two object, such as Worsaw's head, *will* be transmitted by a sub-one transmitter."

"Well, all this has convinced me of one thing."

"And that?" Bridgetta asked.

"I'm just as sure of that, Nathan, and so I have said nothing. One of the few consolations of being here is that I am, for the first time in my life, a free man. I have at last found a way of escaping successfully. The government's first act of assistance would no doubt be to send a crew of men through the transmitters to supervise me here."

"If your luck turned, and Worsaw were to discover you, you'd be thankful for such supervision."

"That's the chance I take."

Hansard shook his head disapprovingly, but by the set of his jaw it was evident that he had decided not to pursue the argument.

"Consider, Nathan, what I have already suffered at the government's hands, and then think if I could gladly invite them *here*. They have taken my invention—which could have made the world a paradise—and turned it into a weapon, as though the world wants for new weapons. I should despair if I thought it were possible for my achievement to be suppressed forever. Happily, as Norbert Wiener observes, the greatest guarantee that a thing will be done is simply the knowledge that it is possible. So that in the long run, unless they prefer annihilation—and they may, they may—my work will not have been for nothing."

There was a long pause during which Hansard considered how most tactfully to protest against Panofsky's apolitical attitude. Didn't the man see the moral necessity of the war? Was he not himself a refugee from the tyranny of East Germany? But before he could formulate these objections clearly, Panofsky had resumed speaking, in a rather more wistful tone.

"Imagine what it might be like. Think what a source of *power* the transmitter represents. The mind staggers. Even *my* mind staggers."

"Of power?" Hansard asked.

"Instead of moving something laterally, suppose one were to transmit it upwards. Water, for instance. A circular waterfall could be created, which could power a dynamo, and only the smallest fraction of the dynamo's power would be needed to operate the transmitter itself. In effect, a perpetual motion machine."

"Then it *does* violate the laws of conservation!"

"At our level of reality, yes. But within the larger system, no. In other words, another universe somewhere is shortly going to experience a considerable power drain. Let us hope they have no means of plugging the hole, eh?"

"My God," said Hansard, who was still envisioning the circular waterfall. "It *would* change everything."

"Everything," Panofsky agreed. "And it will change our view of the universe as well. Not too long ago, in 1600, I regret to say that the Catholic Church burned Giordano Bruno as a heretic. The church will have to change its position now. The universe is infinite, after all; but there is no need for God to be embarrassed on that account. God can simply be *more* infinite. The bigger the universe, the vaster must be God's might. There are, just as Bruno envisioned them, worlds no telescope will ever see; worlds beyond those worlds, worlds still beyond . . . infinities of worlds. Imagine, Nathan, if the earth itself were to be transmitted, and if Earth-Sub-Two were transmitted afterwards, then Earth-Sub-Three. . . . And not just once, but each a dozen, a hundred, numberless times, each transmission producing its own echo."

"Is it possible?"

"Much more is possible, though perhaps not just now. The solar system itself could be transported. We could take our sun with us as we journey about the galaxies. Is it possible? With a transmitter such as this, anything is possible. And what do *you* use it for? What is the only use the military mind can find for such a marvel? To dispense bombs with it!"

"Does the President know about that waterfall-machine you spoke of?"

"Of course he does. It was immediately evident to every scientist in the country that such a thing is possible now."

"Then why isn't it being built? Why, with a source of unlimited power, there never need be a war again—or hunger, or poverty."

"You'll have to answer that question, Captain, for you represent the government, not I."

"You know," said Hansard, unhappily, "perhaps I don't."

TWELVE

THE NATURE OF THE SOUL

"Then you still don't want to tell him about it?" Bridie asked.

"To what end?" Panofsky said. "Why call him back from vacation when there's nothing he can do to alter the situation?"

"He might gather his roses a little more quickly, if he knew," Jet said.

"I think we might best consult the tastes of the lady most directly concerned," said Panofsky, turning to regard Bridgetta, who was now a blonde and no longer, in fact, Bridgetta, but merely Bridget. Her smile spoke for her: *she* was satisfied.

"Any more objections?" Panofsky asked.

"It's best so, of course," said Jet. "It was only selfishness that made me want to share my fear with him. But it becomes harder and harder, as the time advances, to pretend to be lighthearted."

"The effort will be good for both of us," Bridie said. "Pretending makes it so."

"Furthermore," said Panofsky, "we have every reason to suppose it will be called off. The day is fully a month away."

"Not quite that long," corrected his double.

"Well, very nearly a month. After all, it's not as though this were being decided by merely human wit. The best computers in the world are blowing fuses this very minute to do something about it. It's all game theory and bluffing. I, for one, am not worried about it. Not in the least." But when Panofsky's eyes looked across the room and met the eyes of his double, his gaze faltered and his assurance failed.

"Well," said the double somberly, "I, for another, *am*."

Toward the end of Hansard's second week at Elba, and five days after the preceding conversation had taken place our hero found himself doing something he had promised himself never to do again—arguing with his host. Panofsky had made another passing reference to his "little euthanasia program," and Hansard had furrowed his brow just enough to show that he considered it a little murder program; but he steadfastly refused to discuss it.

"It's hardly fair, Nathan, for you to sit in judgment— and Minos himself could not more prominently sit in judgment than you—your face crinkles up like Saran Wrap—and never allow the poor sinner a chance to justify himself, if he can."

"I'll allow that something of the sort has to be done, but . . ."

"But? But? Now, it really isn't fair to stop at that *but*, is it?"

"I was going to say that it seems a perfectly reasonable attitude, from the scientific point-of-view, but it seems strange in a Catholic."

"What a picture you must have of science, Nathan! You pronounce the word as though it were a euphemism for something unspeakable, as if science were the antithesis of the ethical—as, since the bomb, it has in part become."

"I have nothing against the bomb," Hansard protested hastily.

Panofsky allowed this to pass with scarcely the raising of an eyebrow. "But it is curious that you should imagine an opposition between science and Catholicism which, I am sure, you regard as wholly irrational. No? Yes. A dismal prospect, if evil can only be opposed by unreason."

"Honestly, Dr. Panofsky, I don't follow you when you go off on figure-eights like that. What I had in mind was simply this: Catholics are supposed to believe in immortal souls, and that sort of thing. In fact you've already

100

said that you do. But suicide is—I don't know the technical term for it."

"A mortal sin. And so it is, but fortunately I cannot commit that sin at this level of reality. Only Panofsky-Sub-One can commit suicide, in the sense that it's a sin."

"Well, if you take poison and die from it, what else can you call it?"

"First, Nathan, I must explain to you the nature of the soul. At conception, when the soul is created, it is unique, only one, indivisible. God made it so. Do you think *I* can create souls? Of course not. No more can the transmitter, which I invented, create souls. So that the apparent multiplicity of my selves means nothing in God's eyes. I would not go so far as to maintain that I am a mere *illusion*. Rather let us say that I am an epiphenomenon."

"But physically your existence on this plane of reality is just as . . . as existent as it ever was. You breathe. You eat. You *think*."

"Ah, but thinking is not a *soul*. Machines can think."

"Then you're no longer bound by any moral laws whatever?"

"On the contrary, natural law, the law derived from reason as opposed to that which is revealed to us divinely, has as binding a force *here* as in the Real World, just as the laws of physics work *here*. But natural law has always condoned suicide in certain circumstances: consider all those noble Romans throwing themselves on their swords. It is only in these Years of Grace that suicide has become an evil because it is in contradiction to the second supernatural virtue—hope. It is not allowed for a Christian to despair."

"Then you've ceased to be a Christian?"

"I am a Christian perhaps, but not a man. That is to say, the fact that I no longer possess a soul does not prevent me from believing as I always have. I am the same Panofsky as ever, so far as you or I can see, for it is not given to us to see the soul. When Hoffmann sold his soul, he lost his shadow, or was it the other way around? In any case, it was a visible sign. But how much sadder to lose something which one cannot even be sure afterward

101

of having ever possessed. Happily, I am prepared for this paradox by being a modern.

"Camus, you know, was troubled by a similar disparity between the strict atheism which he felt reason required, and his feeling that it was wrong to do evil. But *why* was it wrong? For no reason at all. But still one must have some basis for action, for choosing. So one just tries to do the best one can, from day to day, without examining the ethical dilemma too closely . . . which is more concentration-camp philosophy. I'm sorry I have nothing better to offer you."

"But if it's all meaningless—and isn't that what a soul is all about, meaningfulness?—then why does Panofsky-Sub-One keep providing for you? Why should he care?"

"That is a question that I hope he will never chance to ask himself. Happily, up to now he has devoted all his attention to our physical rather than our spiritual condition. If he were to convince himself that we are soulless, he might very well stop sending us supplies."

"I just can't believe that, Doctor."

"Only because you're not a Catholic."

"Look, if what you said that day in the transmitting room were to happen, if the whole damn world were to be transmitted—what then? With all the people on it, the Pope, everyone?"

"Nathan, what a splendid question! I'd never thought of that. Of course the basic situation remains unaltered, but the *magnitude* of it! A whole *world* without shadows! Yes, and for a final paradox, what if such a transmission were to take place not tomorrow but two thousand years ago, and Christ himself . . . Nathan, you *do* have an instinct for these things. You may have changed my mind, which is an almost unheard-of thing at my age. I will certainly have to give a good deal of thought to the question. But now that I've shown you my soul, such as it is or isn't, would you like to show me yours?"

Hansard's brow furrowed more deeply this time. "I don't understand."

"Why is it, Nathan, that you wake up screaming in the middle of the night?"

And yet another week later.

"I'm sorry," Hansard said, "for flying off the handle with you like that."

"Not with me, I'm afraid," said Panofsky, "though Bernard did tell me about that incident. As a matter of fact, Nathan, I scolded him on your behalf. Your dreams are nobody's business but your own. I think Bernard's let himself become something of a snoop since he left the Real World. That happens to all of us to some degree, but he could confine his eavesdropping to that world and leave *us* alone."

Hansard laughed uneasily. "It's funny you should say that, because I'd just come to tell you—to tell *him*—that he was right. Or, perhaps, not exactly right, but . . ."

"But you were going to answer his question anyhow? Confession does ease the soul, as they say. Especially—I've always observed—the souls of Protestants, in which category I would include those of your stamp. It's because they're so severe with themselves that the fact of mercy overwhelms them."

"I'm not looking for mercy," Hansard said dourly.

"Precisely my point. You'll be all the more surprised to find it. Tell me, Nathan, did you fight in Viet Nam back in the Sixties?"

Hansard turned pale. "I was just about to tell you about that. How did you know?"

"It's nothing telepathic—just a simple inference. If you're thirty-eight now, you would have come of age for the draft at the height of the whole mess. Some very nasty things happened in that war. We civilians with our heads in the sand probably got little idea of what went on, even though the newspapers were full of stories almost every day. Women and children?"

Hansard nodded. "It was a child, a little boy, he couldn't have been much older than five."

"You had to shoot him in self-defense?"

"I incinerated him in self-defense."

They were silent together a long while, though it was not, on Panofsky's part, an unsympathetic silence.

Then Hansard said, reaching for a tone of ordinariness,

"But you knew it all before I even told you. You anticipated everything I had to tell you."

"We sinners are never as unique as we suppose ourselves to be. When a boy of thirteen goes into the confessional with his nails bitten to the quick, the priest will not be surprised to learn that he has committed sins of impurity. When a grown man, an Army captain, who usually evidences the most strait-laced moral code, wakes up screaming in the night, one looks for a cause commensurable to the pain. Also, Nathan, your case is not unique. There have been a dozen novels written about that war by other men who woke up screaming. But why is it, after all this time, you wanted to speak about it?"

"I haven't been able to tell Bridgetta. I tried to, and I couldn't. I thought perhaps I'd be able to, if I told you about it first."

"And why were you anxious to tell her?"

"I've always thought that one of the reasons my first marriage never worked was because I didn't tell Marion about that boy. She wouldn't let me, the one time I tried. This time I won't make that mistake."

"This is news! You're marrying the girl then?"

"In another week. There's going to be a big society wedding at Grace Episcopal, and we thought we'd just sneak in and make it a double wedding. I hope you'll be able to be there to give the bride away."

But before Panofsky could commit himself, Bridie came into the room unannounced and wearing a look of grave concern. "You'd better come and see this, Bernard. We have them on the screen now, and it's just as we feared."

Hansard followed Bridie and Panofsky into the sitting room adjoining Bridgetta's bedchamber. There Bridgetta-Sub-One, in a terrycloth bathrobe and her hair wound up in a towel, was standing a few feet back from the 12-inch screen of the videophone. The Sub-Two residents of Elba were crowded close about another receiver, apparently on an extension line from the first.

The image on the screen that Bridgetta-Sub-One was watching was of Panofsky, but on the other screen there were *two* Panofskys, the second of them with what appeared to be a cloud of cellophane wreathing his head. With the two Panofskys crowded before the screen and the others pictured on it, there were a total of four functioning Panofskys visible to Hansard in a single glance. It was too much, by at least one.

"What in hell is—" he began, but Bridie silenced him with a peremptory gesture.

No sound came from either videophone, but this did not seem to dampen the interest of the spectators. While he waited for this strange charade to end, Hansard reasoned. He reasoned that (1) the videophone that Bridgetta-Sub-One was watching belonged to the Real World (which was confirmable by sticking a finger into it); that (2) the Panofsky pictured upon it must therefore be Panofsky-Sub-One (and hadn't there been talk lately of his having gone off for the Bolshoi's spring season?), and that (3) the *second* Panofsky, visible on the screen of the other videophone (which *was* tangible to Hansard's touch), must be a sublimated Panofsky.

When the call was concluded and the image had shrunk to a small dot of light, Panofsky congratulated Hansard on his reasoning. "One of our knottiest problems," the old man went on, "was establishing communications with the others of us around the world. You see, I've made as much provision as I can for the Sub-Two Panofskys produced by the transmissions from Paris or Moscow back to Washington. There is a gas mask and oxygen supply stored beneath the seat of my wheel chair at all times. It gives me—or him, whichever way you choose to regard it—more or less twenty-four hours' time; enough for one last night at the Bolshoi and sometimes a visit to the Kremlin.

"But of what use is it to be a perfect spy, if one can't communicate what one has unearthed? The method that had to be employed was soon obvious to *us*, but we had to wait for Panofsky-Sub-One to think of it, and sometimes that man can be almost military in his thinking. But at last the solution occurred to him. What we do now is this: At a predetermined time, to be indicated on my desk calendar, Bridgetta-Sub-One receives a call here

105

at Elba from Panofsky-Sub-One who is in another city. Today it was Moscow. Once the connection has been established, it is a simple matter for the Panofsky-Sub-Two then in Moscow to be on hand and give his report at the same time.

"It requires a bit of hithering and thithering on Panofsky-Sub-One's part. Usually he goes from Moscow, after the curtain falls at the Bolshoi, to Paris for supper, and returns to Moscow next day for another performance—and to make the phone call. The sublimated Panofsky does not, of course, appear on the screen of Bridgetta's receiver, but on *this* one, which has itself been sublimated, he does appear. There is no sound, for the Panofsky-Sub-One on the other end has only the air he has brought with him. But we have learned to lip-read, so that is hunky-dory."

"Hunky-dory!" Jet whispered, with a shudder. "*No,* hunky-dory!"

While the first Panofsky sat back to savor his Americanism, the other sighed. "I wish there were some simpler way. This method is so wasteful of lives. There are none of the resources in those other cities that we have here at Elba. It is hard to bring everything one requires for even a short visit. The breathing equipment is bulky, and the secret service guards think it strange that Panofsky-Sub-One should always insist on bringing it along."

"Fortunately," the first Panofsky interrupted (they were neither wearing the skull cap at the moment), "he has a reputation for eccentricity. He has invented a delightfully paranoid theory concerning foreign germs."

The two Panofskys smiled in ironic appreciation of this theory.

"But there are compensations," said the second.

"Oh, yes. There is usually time to see one last performance, and from a vantage better even than the conductor's. Since being sublimated *I* have seen nothing, less than nothing. Here we are in one of the chief cities of the world, the capital of the most affluent culture on earth, and have you ever seen what is called ballet here? It is vomit! I protest against it vehemently. But in Moscow

. . . ah! Tonight, for instance, we were told that Malinova was extraordinary in the second act of *Giselle*."

The second Panofsky sighed more deeply. "Now more than ever does it seem rich to die. For *him,* that is."

"Exactly. *We* shall both be dead inside of two weeks. And *we* will never have seen that *Giselle*. I'd willingly give two weeks of my life to see that."

"Two weeks?" Hansard asked.

"Oh, Bernard!" Bridgetta cried out. "You promised not to say anything."

"My dear, excuse me. It just slipped out."

"Why should you be dead in two weeks?" asked Hansard. "There's something you've been keeping back from me. I've felt it in the air ever since I came here."

"May I tell him?" Panofsky inquired of Bridgetta.

"What choice is there now? Nathan, don't look like that. I didn't want you to know, because . . . because we were so happy."

"In two weeks, Captain Hansard, all hell breaks loose. To be precise, on the first of June. My double in Moscow just informed us that the Kremlin is being as foolishly resolute and resolutely foolish as Washington."

"I find that hard to believe," said Hansard.

"Nevertheless, it is so. Bridgetta, may I show him the letter?"

"Try to understand, Mr. Hansard," Bridie said (for Bridgetta, in tears now, was able to do no more than nod her head yes), "that when Bridget followed you that day and took this out of its hiding place in the Monument, she was only concerned to find out who you were. We had no way of knowing if we could trust you. We weren't expecting anything of this sort."

"You mean to say you opened that attaché case? But it was Priority-A!"

Panofsky removed a folded paper from his coat pocket and handed it to Hansard. "The case contained only this letter, Nathan. And since this letter was signed, a month ago, nothing has altered."

After he had digested the President's written order, after he had convinced himself of its authenticity, Hansard said, "But the diplomats . . . Or the United Nations . . ."

"No," said Jet dismally. "I've been watching them here in Washington every day. The President, the Secretary of Defense, the Russian ambassador—none of them will unbend. Because CASS-9 won't. They've become the slaves of that computer. And now the President and the Cabinet and all the important officers of the Pentagon have gone into hiding. They've been away for a week . . . It bodes no good."

"I simply can't believe that if nobody *wants* the war—"

"Has anybody *ever* wanted the war? But it was bound to happen, you know. The whole effectiveness of our arsenal as a deterrent force was based on the possibility of it being used. Now that possibility will be realized."

"But there's been no aggression, no provocation . . . !"

"CASS-9, apparently, does not need to be provoked. I'll confess that, with respect to game theory, I am naïve."

The second Panofsky, who had been listening intently the while, hit the arm of his wheel chair with his fist and swore.

"He is so especially distressed," his double explained, "because he knows he could stop it. If only there were a way for him to speak to Panofsky-Sub-One."

"If all that you say is true, though," Hansard said, deliberately, "it seems to be too late for the explanations of men of good will."

"You mistake my meaning, Nathan. He, Bernard Panofsky, singlehanded, could stop the war—snap! like that. It is all written out on vellum; a splendid, magnificent preposterous plan. But it cannot be carried through by any of us, only by someone of the Real World. And so it is all no good, a failure. . . ."

"Singlehanded?" Hansard asked, with a note of professional incredulity.

"Alas, yes," said both Panofskys in chorus.

Then one of them removed the skull cap from his pocket and put it on his head. "If you please, Bernard— *I* will tell him how."

THIRTEEN

MARS

Here there were no usual measures of time. The Camp lived on a twenty-four-hour earth-day; but a complete rotation of Mars took thirty-six minutes longer, so that only once in forty days was the high noon of the sun in perfect agreement with the high noon dictated by the clocks on the wall.

Five weeks of anxious waiting had slipped by in a twinkling. Five weeks in a limbo of inactivity and the ritual gesturing of the run-throughs and inspections. Five weeks going up and down the olive-drab corridors, eating tinfoil dinners, swilling hot coffee, thinking the same well-worn thoughts which, through repetition (just as the food seemed to lose its flavor day by day), grew wearisome and were set aside.

Like a spring brook in the dry season of the year, conversation subsided to a trickle. The enlisted men passed the long hours with endless poker games. General Pittmann kept more and more to himself, and so, perforce, did Captain Hansard.

A strange condition, a condition difficult to describe except in negatives. Life was reduced to a minimum of automatic processes—waking, sleeping, eating, walking here and there, watching the time slip by, listening to silences. The Camp's narrow world of rooms and corridors came to seem somehow . . . unreal.

Or was it himself that seemed so? He had read a story once, or seen a movie, of a man who sold his shadow— or perhaps it was his reflection in a mirror. Hansard felt like that now—as though at the moment of the Mars jump five weeks before, he had lost some essential, if intangible, part of himself. A soul perhaps, though he didn't exactly believe he had one.

He wished that the countermand to the President's order would come, but he wished even more that he might be called back to the fuller reality of earth. Yet these were neither very strong wishes, for the reservoirs of all desire were drying up within him. He wished mainly for an ending, any ending, an event to accent this drear, uninflected, trickling time.

So perhaps there had been a sort of wisdom behind the decision to keep the men at the Mars Command Posts two months at a stretch, even though there was no technical necessity for it, the same wisdom that is at the root of all the compulsory dullness of military life. For boredom makes a soldier that much more able and that much more willing to perform the task that it is especially given a soldier to perform.

Ex-Sergeant John Worsaw sat in the guard bay before the door to the control room reading a tattered personalized novel. Because of his reading habits, Worsaw had a reputation around Camp Jackson/Mars as an intellectual. This was an exaggeration, of course. But, as he liked to point out in his more ponderous moments (after about two beers), you couldn't get anywhere in the year 1990 without brains, and brains wouldn't do you much good either—without an education. (Worsaw had earned a College Equivalent Diploma in Technics.) Take Wolf Smith, for example, the Army chief of staff. That was a man who had more facts at his command than a CASS-9 computer. For a man like Smith, facts were like ammunition.

Facts. Worsaw had nothing but contempt for people who couldn't face hard facts. Like that fairy Pittmann in the control room now, worrying about the bombs probably, and afraid of the button. No one had told Worsaw of the President's order, but he knew what was in the air by the looks on the two officers' faces. What were they scared about, as long as they were here on Mars? It was the sons of bitches back on earth who had to worry!

Thinking something to this effect, though rather more hazily, Worsaw found that he had read down a quarter of a page of the novel without taking any of it in. With a more concentrated effort, he returned to the last passage he remembered:

Worsaw lobbed another grenade in the bunker entrance and threw himself flat, pressing his face into the jungle dirt. Thunder rent the air, and thick yellow smoke belched from the crumbling structure.

"That oughta do it, Snooky!" yelled the corporal, thumbing the safety off his M-14. "Let's mop up now." And Corporal O'Grady leaped to his feet.

"Look out, Lucky!" Even as Worsaw screamed, it was too late. The sniper bullets had caught O'Grady in a vicious cross-fire, spinning him and flinging him mudward, a dead man.

"The yellow-belly sons of bitches," Worsaw muttered. "They'll pay for this!"

A few feet away the blood of Lucky O'Grady seeped out into the jungle soil. The man who had been Worsaw's best friend had run out of luck at last.

Strangely moved by this last paragraph, Worsaw laid his book aside. He had heard someone coming down the corridor, and it was likely, at this hour of the day, with the men playing cards in their barracks, to be Hansard. The captain spent a lot of his time roaming about in the corridors.

"General Pittmann?"

"Yes, he's inside, sir."

Hansard went into the control room, closing the door after him. Worsaw cursed him softly; but there was in that quiet obscenity a trace of respect, even affection. Despite the pressure to restore his rank that Worsaw had put on him through Ives (who owed Worsaw more than a few favors and could be counted on to pay his debt), Hansard wasn't backing down. Which showed guts. Worsaw admired guts.

But the deeper motive of Worsaw's admiration was simply that he knew Hansard to be a veteran of Viet Nam, the last of the big fighting wars. Worsaw himself had been born four years too late to enlist for that war and so he had never, to his chagrin, undergone a soldier's baptism by fire. He had never known, and now perhaps he never would, what it was like to look at a man through the sights of a loaded rifle, squeeze the trigger and see that man fall dead. Life had cheated Worsaw of that supreme experience, and it had offered very little by way of compensation. Why else, after all, does a person go Army?

He fished the novel out of his back pocket and started to read again. He skipped ahead to the chapter he liked best, the burning of the village of Tam Chau. The anonymous author described it very well, with lots of convincing details. Worsaw liked a realistic-type novel that showed what life was like.

FOURTEEN

THE BRIDE

Love will intrude itself into places where it simply has no business to be—into lives or stories that are just too occupied with other matters to give it its due. But somehow it can always be squeezed in. Marriage is an exemplary institution for this purpose, because conjugal love can usually "go without saying," whereas the more exotic forms of romance demand the stage all to themselves, scornful of the ordinary business of life. A married man can divide his life comfortably in half, into a private and a public sector which need never, so long as both run smoothly along, impinge upon each other.

Thus Hansard had fallen in love, paid court, proposed, been accepted, and now it is the very morning of the wedding—and all these things have already taken place, as it were, in the wings. We should not suppose, because of this, that Hansard's was a milder sort of love than another man's, or that the romance was so ordinary and undistinguished as to be without interest for us—or even, perhaps, for the principals involved. We need only point out the singular circumstance that the rivals of the beloved were essentially her exact doubles to dispel such a notion.

No, if there were time, it would be most interesting to linger over their month-long idyll, to document the days and nights, to smile at the follies, to record the quick-silver weathers of their growing love. For instance, notice how Hansard's expression has relaxed. There is a sparkle in his eyes that we have not seen there before. Or is it, perhaps, that they seem deeper? He smiles more often—there can be no doubt of that; and even when he is not smiling there is something about his lips . . . what is it? Do they seem fuller now? See, too, how his jaw has relaxed, and when he turns his head how the tendons are less prominent. Small changes, but taken as a whole they give his face an altogether different stamp. Surely it is a change for the better.

Already it is May 26, the morning of the wedding. How quickly a month can go by! And is there no time left to tell how splendid a month it has been, or what has been happening back there in the wings? By all means, let us take the time, while the bride and her three bridesmaids (for Bridgetta-Sub-One had gone through the transmitter once more, increasing the Sub-Two population by one; and the newcomer immediately assumed the role of Bridget, for the bride would now be neither Bridie nor Jet nor yet Bridget, but Mrs. Hansard), the two Panof-skys, and Hansard are walking down the May-morning streets to the church.

The month had gone by as though they'd been playing a game all the while. There had been such *fun*. Some-times Hansard spent the day alone with "his" Bridgetta; at other times one or more of her doubles would come out with them to "swim" in the municipal police station or in the Senate buildings. He and Bridgetta had made love in heaps of flowers in a florist's window. They had taken picnic lunches to diplomatic dinners where, because there was no room for them around the table, they had sat on top and dangled their legs through the tablecloth.

They'd played tennis, singles and doubles, after spread-ing slices of the linoleum rugs about the court so that they wouldn't lose the tennis balls. The greatest lark, once Hansard got over his embarrassment at playing a child's game, had been Bridgetta's special version of hide-and-seek which they played in the most crowded streets and offices of the city while the sober workaday population milled about them.

They'd sneaked into the most expensive theatres and left during the first act if they found the play not to their liking—left without any regret for the money wasted. (And, more often than not, the plays were boring because they had to be seen in dumb show.) At especially bad performances, Hansard and one or more Bridgettas would get up on the stage and ham it up themselves.

Such fun, and much, much more, too; gentler moments that might be only a word, a caress, a glance, forgotten as quickly as it happened. But what, if not the sum of such moments, is love? A moment, a month—how quickly —and here they are already on the way to the church!

The bride was wearing a makeshift gown sewn together from damask tablecloths and synthetic lace plundered from various articles of lingerie, no one back in the Real World having had the forethought, or the occasion, to provide for such a contingency as this today. If only fashion were considered, the bridesmaids might have been thought a good deal better dressed than the bride. But the bride was wrapped in the glory of a myth that quite out-tops all that fashion can do.

Both Panofskys were wearing formal clothes, because they had usually set off through the transmitters attired formally for the theatre. Hansard, however, had nothing better than his everyday uniform, for which the hat was still missing.

The church was crowded when they arrived, and there was no room for the invisible intruders except before the altar. Bridie put a tape of the *Tannhäuser* wedding march on the portable phonograph and let it play at medium volume. There was a stir in the waiting crowd, and heads turned to regard the bride advancing down the center aisle, her train borne up by three children. "A pity we

114

couldn't get orange blossoms for you, my dear," Panofsky whispered to the bride-to-be, who was holding a bouquet of yesterday's wilted roses, the transmitters of Elba having provided nothing more appropriate for the day.

Bridgetta took three steps forward to stand behind the other bride, her feet planted squarely in the billowing train. The two grooms came out of the sacristy to take the hands of their betrotheds. The minister began to speak the silent words of the ceremony, which Panofsky, reading his lips, repeated after him.

Hansard had to dodge out of the way when the groom reached around to receive the ring from his best man. Panofsky handed Hansard the ring that Bridie had made from a costume-jewelry ring of her own by removing the stone and filing away the setting until there was only a thin gold band. Hansard placed the gold circlet on Bridgetta's finger.

He leaned forward to kiss her. When his lips were almost touching hers, she whispered, "Say it again," and he said, "*I do, I do!*" Then they kissed, man and wife now, till death should part them.

"I've written a small epithalamion for the occasion. Would anyone like to hear a small epithalamion?" Panofsky asked.

"Afterward. Epithalamions come with the dinner," Jet said.

The sub-one bride and groom turned around and, stepping to invisible music, descended from the altar and went out of the church. Bridie · ran the tape ahead to the sprightlier Mendelssohn theme. Hansard and Bridgetta stopped kissing.

"Stand back, and let me look at you," he said, smiling broadly.

She stepped back, and then, when the shot rang out, stepped back again. Blood stained the makeshift bridal gown just beneath her heart. Her mouth dropped open, and the smile was vanished from her lips, from her eyes. He caught her in his arms. *She was dead.*

"That's *one*," shouted a half-familiar voice. Hansard turned to see Worsaw standing in the midst of the wedding

115

guests crowding into the aisle. "And this is two." The rifle fired again, but he missed Bridie, who had been his second target.

"Get down, out of sight!" Hansard shouted, though he did not think to take his own advice. Jet took hold of the wheel chair of one Panofsky and pushed him into the sacristy. Bridie and the new Bridget both dove into the floor. The other Panofsky had driven off under his own power and Hansard could not see him, though indeed he could see very little beyond the widening circle of blood staining the damask of the bridal dress. Forgotten, the tape recorder continued to play the Mendelssohn march tune.

"Beast!" Panofsky's voice shouted. "Monstrous, loveless beast!" He was driving his wheel chair through the crush of people in the center aisle. He aimed a revolver at Worsaw, but even from where he was Hansard could see the old man's aim was wide. A third and fourth shot rang out, the pistol and then the rifle, and Panofsky pitched forward in his chair. The wheels penetrated the surface of the floor, but the chair scarcely slowed in its headlong motion forward. Soon the wheel chair, bearing the crumpled body, had passed out of sight downward.

Hansard realized that the moment demanded action, but he was reluctant to let his bride's still-warm body sink to the floor.

Another rifle shot, and the tape recorder was silenced.

"That was dumb, Hansard," Worsaw called out. "Playing that music was plain dumb. I wouldn't of known you was in here without that."

Gently, Hansard lowered Bridgetta's body, keeping his eyes always on her murderer.

"Oh, you don't have to worry yourself yet, Captain. I won't touch *you* till I've wiped out your friends. I've got a score to settle with you. Remember?"

Hansard reached inside the jacket of his uniform for the pistol with which Panofsky had provided him. He did not move fast.

"Don't be stupid, Captain. How can you pull that out, when all I have to do is squeeze a trigger? Now put your

116

hands up in the air, and tell those women and that other old man to come out from where they're hiding. If they're good-looking enough, I might not have to kill them after all. How about that?"

Hansard did not obey these commands, nor did he, by any deliberate action, disobey them. Indeed, his mind was too numb to produce the thoughts that would have led him to action.

Behind Worsaw a woman's voice let forth an incoherent cry; Worsaw spun to face the imagined danger, but it came not from behind him, as it first seemed, but from above. He had been standing at the back of the church, beneath the choir loft. When he turned, Panofsky's wheel chair dropped through the low-hanging ceiling on top of him. Hansard's wits thawed sufficiently for him to draw his pistol from its holster and empty it into Worsaw's back.

Jet dropped down from the choir loft and came running forward to Hansard. She spoke disjointedly. "I thought . . . are you hurt? . . . and then, around the outside of the church, and up the stairs to the choir . . . it was so heavy, and I could hear him. . . ." He allowed her to embrace him, but he did not return her embrace. His body was rigid, his jaw tense, his eyes glazed with a film of inexpressivity.

Once she'd released him he walked forward and turned over Worsaw's bleeding body. "Three times," he said. "First, inside the manmitter. Then, at the pumping station, and now here. I seem to spend all my time killing this one man."

Bridie and the new Bridget came in at the main door, where the last of the wedding guests were filing out. "Bernard is dead," Bridie announced. "We found him in the cellar. But where's the other Bernard?"

"In the sacristy," said Jet. "Hiding in the minister's clothes closet. It was his idea that I use his chair as a projectile. He felt that I would probably have just as poor aim with a pistol as his double had."

"I seem to spend all my *life* killing people," Hansard said aloud, though he seemed to be talking only to himself.

"Nathan, it isn't like that," Jet insisted earnestly. "What happened today could have happened any time, without your ever being around. It was an accident; a grotesque accident."

"Go away, please, all of you. I'd rather not see . . . your faces . . . when hers . . ." He turned away from the three women and walked back to the altar. There he took up the dead Bridgetta in his arms.

Jet would have protested again, but she was checked by Bridie. Instead she went with the empty wheel chair into the sacristy. Bridie and the new Bridget dragged the body of Worsaw out of the church. In five minutes Jet returned to ask when they would see him again.

"I want to spend the night here," Hansard said, "with my bride."

Jet went away. The cleaning people came into the church and began to sweep it out and mop up, though they did not see the blood-flecked book lying in the center aisle: *The Private War of Sergeant Worsaw*.

Afterward, the electric lights were turned off. In the semidarkness Hansard found himself able at last to cry. It had been many years since the tears had come from those eyes, and they did not, at first, flow freely.

Before the brute fact of death nothing can be said. It would be best if, like the three women, we leave Hansard to himself now. His grief, like his love, cannot take a very large part in our story—which is not very far from ending.

FIFTEEN

WOLFGANG AMADEUS MOZART

And yet, what a curious, contradictory grief it was. For she who had died was not dead. She was alive; thrice over she was alive. Though no one of the Bridgettas proposed this consolation in so many words, still the daily and unavoidable fact of their presence—of *her* presence—could

118

not but have its effect on Hansard. In one sense, it only made his loss more poignant by offering constant reminders of her whom he had lost. On the other hand he could not very well pretend that his loss was irreplaceable.

The surviving Panofsky and three Bridgettas, for their part, accepted what had happened with great equanimity. They were, after all, accustomed to the idea of their own expendability.

Then too there was the sobering consideration that in a week—in six days—in five days—they would *all* be dead; Bridgetta, Panofsky, Hansard, and the whole populace of the Real World. Even in the depths of his grief Hansard was aware of the minutes slipping by, of the dreaded day creeping up on them like a fog bank rolling in from the river.

On the evening of the 27th, Panofsky called them all together. "The question arises, fellow citizens, how shall we pass the time? Bridgetta has a supply of LSD in our medicine cabinet, should anyone so desire."

Hansard shook his head no.

"Nor do I. However, we may change our mind. If anyone starts to panic, it's a good thing to remember. I understand it's especially helpful for terminal cancer patients, and somehow I've always associated cancer with the bomb. There are also any number of bottles of good brandy and Scotch in the cellar, should the need arise. What I would suggest, most seriously, is what a defrocked priest advised in a clandestine religion class in the labor camp of my youth—that if one knows the Day of Judgment is at hand, one should just go about one's ordinary business. Any other course partakes of hypocrisy. For my own part, I intend to study the folio of equations that Bernard-Sub-One has just sent me through the transmitter."

Though it was sensible advice, Hansard had difficulty following it. With Bridgetta dead, the ordinary fabric of his life had dissolved. He might still continue to mourn her, but as the time advanced, the magnitude of the impending catastrophe seemed to mock at the smallness of his own sorrow. Perhaps it was exactly this that goaded

119

him to find a solution to the catastrophe, and thereby restore a measure of dignity to his own mourning.

Or perhaps it was just luck.

However that may be, he found himself more and more driven to listen to music. At first he gave his attention to the more fulsomely elegiac selections from Panofsky's library of tapes: *Das Lied von der Erde, Die Winterreise,* the *Missa Solemnis.* He listened to the music with an urgency more intense than he had known even at the depth of his adolescent *Sturm-und-Drang;* as though some part of him already knew that the key he sought was concealed behind these silvery shifting tone-fabrics, hidden in the pattern but a part of it.

Gradually he found the Romantics, even Beethoven, too heavy for his taste. He would have liked to turn to Bach then, but Panofsky's library provided only the Sonatas for Unaccompanied Violin and the Well-Tempered Clavier. Here too, though still indistinctly, he felt the presence moving just beyond the veil; yet when he tried to touch it, to fix it firmly in apprehension it eluded him as when, reaching into a pool of water, the fish dart swiftly out of reach of the grasping hand. At last it was Mozart who gave it to him.

On the first play-through of the tape of *Don Giovanni,* he felt the veil tearing. It began during the trio of the three masquers at the end of the first act, and the rent widened steadily until the penultimate moment when Donna Elvira arrives to interrupt the Don at his carousal. He scorns her earnest warnings; she turns to go out the door . . . and screams; the great D-minor chord thunders in the orchestra, and the statue bursts into the hall to drag the unrepentant Don to hell.

Hansard stopped the tape, reversed the reel, and listened to the scene again from the moment of Donna Elvira's scream.

The veil parted.

"The *chord,*" he said. "Of course, *the chord.*"

He tore himself away from the music to seek out

Panofsky, but discovered the old man sitting only a few feet away, listening raptly to the opera.

"Doctor Panofsky, I—"

"Please, the music! And no more of that foolish 'Doctor.' "

Hansard switched off the recorder during the height of the brief, electric scene between Don Giovanni and the statue.

"I'm sorry, but I must tell you now. It concerns the music, in a way—but more than that, I've thought of how it can be done . . . what you said could not be . . . how to communicate with the Real World! Perhaps, just perhaps."

"The most awesome moment in all music, and you—"

"I'll form a chord!"

"It is true," Panofsky replied, in a more moderate tone, "that Mozart can suggest to us a harmony embracing the world; but art, sadly, is not the same thing as reality. You are wrought up, Nathan. Calm yourself."

"No, no, truly—*this is the way!* You *can* talk to Panofsky-Sub-One by becoming part of him again, by restoring the unity that was disrupted. You'll mesh with his body—and with his mind; probably when he's asleep."

A light began to glow in Panofsky's eyes. "I am a fool," he whispered, then paused, as though waiting for Hansard to contradict him—or perhaps for his other self to agree. He went on: "An idiot. A chord—yes, it is a fine analogy, though, mind you, nothing *more*. I can't be sure yet. There is a demonstrable relationship between a man of the Real World and his echo, a sort of proportion, but whether it is enough . . . I cannot, in the time we have left, develop a mathematical model . . ."

"There's no need to. Just *do* it!"

"But what a lovely analogy." Panofsky's eyes were closed, and his fingers moved in pantomime before him. "You sound middle C on the piano, and simultaneously the C an octave above. The ear can no longer sort out what it hears, and the overtones of the two notes resolve into a single chord."

121

"The fibers of the body would be the overtones," Hansard theorized eagerly. "The tone of the muscles, the memory traces of the brain, the blood type, the whole pattern of being. Place the two patterns together, and there'll be a sort of resonance between them, a knitting together."

"Yes, a kind of understanding, perhaps; a natural sympathy, a bond."

"A chord . . . And wouldn't communication be posble then?"

"Without evidence, Nathan, how can we know? But there's a chance, and I must try it. If it works—why then, Nathan, you and I may have saved the world at its last minute. You frown! What now, Nathan? Is it that you misdoubt my plan? Well, well, Napoleon had his skeptics too, and see how far he went.

"No, I'm perfectly confident that once I've been able to communicate with Panofsky-Sub-One I can carry it off, grandiloquent as it must sound to you. But now I must find that gentleman out. And—speak of the devil . . ."

For another Panofsky had just entered the library through the open door. "You *might* have been waiting outside the transmitter if you'd been expecting me. It wasn't very cheery coming into an empty house. Why are the two of you looking at me as though I were a ghost? And for that matter—" turning to Hansard, "I don't believe we've been introduced."

"But you're not Panofsky-Sub-One," Hansard said.

"A sound induction. No, *he* just left for Moscow. Didn't you see where I'd noted it down on the memo calendar?"

"And Bridgetta?" his double asked.

"Went with him, of course."

"How long will they be gone?"

"Till June 2nd, when Malinova repeats her *Giselle*. Good heavens, Bernard, what's the matter? You look as though I'd just announced the end of the world."

But, a little later:

"You can't expect me to *build* it!" Hansard protested.

"Nonsense, Nathan, there's nothing to build. Just a trifle

122

f rewiring. Surely there is a stock of spare elements at
he Mars base. With the equipment as it exists, it shouldn't
ake more than fifteen minutes' work to convert those
lements to what we'll need."

"But the elements for the Camp Jackson manmitter are
o small!"

"Size is no consideration, Nathan, nor is distance. And
ou'll have all the power you need in a dry cell. No, my
hief worry is not in your assembling the transmitter, but
1 your getting the co-ordinates down pat. I think we can
fford a day of practice. Have you ever put together your
wn hi-fi?"

"When I was a kid."

"Then you should have no trouble. A hi-fi is more com-
licated. Let me show you what you must do. In the lab-
ratory. Now. Quickly, quickly!"

At twilight on the 29th of May Hansard and Bridie
:ood once again on Gove Street and watched the men
f Camp Jackson walking in and out of the wall about
1e pumping station. Their number had been much re-
uced: Hansard counted fewer than ten. It was necessary
) use these transmitters, which were in continuous oper-
tion, rather than the manmitters within the camp proper
nce there were no jumps scheduled to Camp Jackson/
1ars for two more weeks. Had Panofsky possessed the
)-ordinates for the Mars Command Post, Hansard might
ave foregone this sort of hitchhiking altogether.

Finally the last of the men they had seen go in came
ack out. They waited another half hour, then strolled
own the street to the wall and through it, trundling an
mpty wheel chair before them. The door of the pumping
ouse had been standing open during the day, and the
reat volume of sub-two water had spilled out, to run
own the hill and form a shallow moat on the inside of
1e wall. There were only a few inches of water on the
oor of the station, and the steady cascade pouring out
f the transmitter—the echo of the water that had just
:en transmitted to Mars. A chilly breeze stirred their
othing, originating in the transmitting chamber of the
r pump.

"Now," Bridie said briskly, "we shall just have to hope that we can discover to which of the Posts they're transmitting at any given moment. Follow the technicians about and see what they do. Meanwhile, I'll look over the equipment."

Within five minutes they had found the switch marked CJ that controlled air transmissions. They observed two full cycles of transmission as the stream of air was routed to each of the Command Posts in turn; there was an interval between transmissions averaging five seconds. Only during this time would it be safe for Hansard to enter the transmitting chamber; a little earlier or a little later, and he would be transmitted piecemeal to Mars, as Worsaw had been.

"It's not enough time," Bridie said unhappily.

"It's enough time," Hansard said.

They took turns blowing up the air mattress that was to serve as his cushion inside the transmission chamber. The cushion was not for the sake of comfort but to prevent as much as possible, any part of Hansard from projecting through the "floor" of the chamber and being left behind.

Hansard began to strap on the breathing equipment that had been stored on the underside of Panofsky's wheel chair. There would not be sub-two air on Mars, so he would have to bring his own supply. He pulled the flimsy-looking clear plastic mask down over his head, sealed it about his neck, and opened the valve controlling oxygen input.

"Ready or not," he said, "here I come." Only after the words had left his lips did he realize that they had been an unconscious echo of his games of hide-and-seek with Bridgetta.

Bridie said something, but with the mask sealed over his head he could not hear her. She stepped directly before him and repeated the words, with exaggerated movements of her lips and appropriate gestures: "We . . LoVe . . . You."

Hansard nodded curtly. "Ditto," he whispered.

Bridie stood on tiptoe so she might kiss him. Their lips pressed against each other's through the thin film of plastic.

"Be . . . LucKy . . . CoMe . . . BacK."

He positioned himself before the transmitting chamber, nd Bridie watched over the shoulder of the technician rowing switches. She nodded to Hansard, who carefully id the rubber mattress on the bottom of the chamber, en, sliding in through the thin metal wall, spread him-elf out flat on it in the darkness. In almost the same in-tant the mattress popped and the air rushed out. "Hell!" Iansard said aloud, but it was too late to turn back now. t almost any moment the switch would be thrown that ould send him to Mars.

It was taking too long. He remembered the last time he ad gone through a transmitter—the long wait, the hand oming through the door of the vault. . . .

Then he realized that he was there, that the mattress ad popped at the moment of transmission. Some part of : had been pushed down through the floor of the cham-er, outside the field of transmission. It was fortunate for Iansard that it had been the mattress that had thus nadvertently punctured and not his gas mask.

He rose to his feet and walked forward in the darkness f the receiving chamber. He came to a wall, passed hrough it. There, not ten feet away, drinking coffee with ieneral Pittmann, was Nathan Hansard, Captain in the Jnited States Army. No man had ever seemed more trange to Hansard than he.

The mattress popped and the air rushed out. "Hell!" Iansard said aloud, but it was too late to turn back now. 'hen his sub-three flesh, too insubstantial to be supported y the "skin" of energy of the sub-one world (Mars, ot earth, since this transmitter, unlike the Camp Jackson nanmitter, transmitted continuously, re-echoing endlessly he echoes thrown back by transmission), began to sink lowly into the ground. Realizing the hopelessness of his ituation, Hansard-Sub-Three turned off the oxygen input alve.

An infinite series of Nathan Hansards—echoes of echoes —made the same decision, and each died clinging to the ame hope: "I hope he makes it."

SIXTEEN

THE CHORD

"You're not looking well, Nathan. Small wonder. I don't suppose I look very thriving myself."

As a matter of fact, though, that was just how one would have described General Pittmann at that moment: thriving. While Hansard had seemed to age a decade in these last weeks, the General's features had assumed a strange and unbecoming youthfulness, an effect exaggerated by an unaccustomed looseness in his manner.

His tie was knotted lopsidedly, and his collar unbuttoned. His hair needed trimming, and his shoes were scuffed. There was a lightness in his step, a nervousness in his gestures, a quickness in his speech, that had not been customary to him these many years. Just so, the weather of an October afternoon can sometimes be mistaken for spring.

Hansard looked down at the rainbow-banded swirls of oil coating his coffee. With great effort he moved his lips to say, "No, sir."

"Perhaps you're not getting enough vitamins. I notice that you've been missing meals. We should always take care of our health. Good health is our most precious possession."

Hansard couldn't decide if the General was taunting him with these banalities, or if he really did have so little sense of their inappropriateness.

"Now if I were Julius Caesar, I would be wary of someone with that 'lean and hungry look' of yours."

A joke seemed to be called for, so Hansard roused himself to make an attempt. "I'd lose that look fast enough, if you could get us something to eat besides these everlasting frozen dinners."

Pittmann's laughter was out of proportion to the joke

He indulged himself in a short diatribe against Army food. It was quite funny, and despite himself Hansard had to smile. Since it had become evident, two weeks before, that the orders were not going to be countermanded, neither man had mentioned the bombs.

Hansard$_2$ regarded himself with something approaching horror. That wan smile, those furtive eyes returning ever and again to the coffee cup, the pallor and inertness of his flesh and, overwhelmingly, his *falseness*. For though he could not understand what words Hansard$_1$ was speaking, he knew, beyond all doubt, that they were lies.

At twenty-one-hundred-thirty hours Hansard$_1$ finished his coffee and went out into the corridor, Hansard$_2$ following, where he strolled idly and ill-at-ease. Hansard$_2$ experienced another moment of uncanniness when on his way out of the toilet he passed Worsaw, who, when he saw that Hansard$_1$ could no more see him, sneered and muttered a silent obscenity that did not need a lip reader to interpret.

How strange it seemed that this man, resenting him as deeply as he did, should yet be subservient to him here. How had society so been ordered that all mankind should accept the invisible restraints of custom—Hansard no less than Worsaw? For it was evident that Hansard$_1$, for no more compelling reason than because it was expected of him, was prepared to assist at the annihilation of humanity in violation of everything he knew to be moral. It was a paltry consolation to realize that a million others could have been found as pliable as he.

Eventually Hansard$_1$ went into his own small room which, despite some few shards of blond wool tentatively posing as furniture, seemed less a habitation than a branch of the corridor that came to a dead end here. Instead of preparing for sleep, Hansard$_1$ took a book from the wall locker and began to read.

It was the Bible. Hansard had not looked into a Bible since he'd prepared for Confirmation a quarter of a century before. This nervous, morose stranger seemed to bear less and less relationship with anyone Hansard$_2$ could recognize as himself.

It had seemed worth a try. Wasn't religion intended for just such times as this, when all reasonable hopes were daunted? "Though I walk through the valley of the shadow of death—" and all that.

But it wasn't working. For one thing, there was just so much of it, and none that he had found—neither prophets nor apostles nor yet the faded image of Christ, who seemed to live, for Hansard, in a landscape of calendar art—seemed quite to the purpose. Here on death's brink he found it as hard to believe in the Resurrection and the Life as he had at the age of fourteen when, for his parents' sake (and had *they* really cared so much themselves?), he had been confirmed.

No, he had found no consolation here, but he did—as one will torment oneself by probing at a rotten tooth— take a kind of perverse pleasure in reading just those passages in *Job,* in *Ecclesiastes,* in *Jeremiah,* that strengthened and confirmed his unbelief:

Then said I in my heart: As it happeneth to the fool, so it happeneth even to me; and why was I then more wise? Then I said in my heart, that this also is vanity.

For there is no remembrance of the wise more than of the fool for ever; seeing that which now is in the days to come shall all be forgotten. And how dieth the wise man? As the fool.

Therefore I hated life; because the work that is wrought under the sun is grievous unto me; for all is vanity and vexation of spirit.

In sleep the complex melodies of conscious thought would be dampened; there would be only the simple C of Hansard$_1$'s sleeping mind and, an octave below, the C of Hansard$_2$. Such, at least, had been his hope. But he was impatient.

Now, he thought, *it may be possible. . . .*

Carefully he lowered his frame into the seated body of

Hansard$_1$. A curious and not quite pleasant sensation to feel his two legs, real and ghostly, slipping into alignment, to feel his breath stop for a moment and then return, synchronized with the breathing of Hansard$_1$. His vision blurred, and then, when it was restored, he found his eyes moving over the printed page, not reading, only seeing the print skitter past.

He concentrated on the meaning of the text and tried to bend his mind to the emotional state that he supposed must be Hansard$_1$'s. But though he could feel his larynx vibrating with the same subvocalized sound patterns, the two minds maintained their distinct identities. Sometimes he would feel a memory stirring with strange autonomy, or he would feel, fleetingly, the most inexpressible sadness. But it was with these moments, as with night-vision, that whenever he tried to concentrate on them they would retire into the obscurity whence they had come.

Reluctantly he disengaged himself from Hansard$_1$. It was no good. He would have to wait till he went to sleep.

Hansard could not sleep. Since he had made the Mars jump he had been taking heavier and heavier dosages of barbiturates, but they no longer helped. He lay on his bunk in the darkness, remembering how, as a child, in another darkness, he had lain awake so, trying by sheer power of imagination to place himself outside his slum-suburban bedroom and far far off—on Mars, perhaps—whispering—*If I pretend hard enough it will come true.*

And so it had; so it had.

Now where? Now what worlds could he wish himself away to? Madness, perhaps; such madness as seemed to have possessed Pittmann. Or sleep? But he remembered a line from Shakespeare: "To sleep, perchance to dream—aye, there's the rub."

He elbowed himself out of bed, smoothed the wrinkles out of his shirt, and went out into the corridor. Now where?

In the observatory he looked at the dead rocks of Mars. In his youth, he had been so sure that Mars was teeming with life. Even when the first Mariner pictures came back (he had been thirteen) he refused to believe them. Nobody believes, at that age, that there can be such a thing as death.

Though the clocks inside the Command Post gave the time as only a bit after midnight it was a bright, chiaroscuro morning outside. It hurt one's eyes to look too long upon it.

Sleep, you bastard, sleep! Hansard$_2$ thought angrily. He did not dare cease pacing the floor of the observatory, for he was himself so tired (having kept himself awake throughout the previous night just so he would not be insomniac himself) as to be in danger of dropping off to sleep if he let himself sit down anywhere. Hansard$_1$, meanwhile, sat staring at the Mars noonday. What in that barren waste absorbed him so?

At length Hansard$_1$ returned to his room and lay down again, without undressing. In the utter darkness Hansard$_2$ had no way to know if his double had fallen asleep, except by entering his body.

This time Hansard$_1$'s eyes were closed. His jaw relaxed, his mouth opened slightly, his lungs drew deeper breaths of air.

His fist unclenched, and he accepted the case of ammunition that was handed to him. They were going hunting. "For what?" he asked, but the grownups went on chattering in their shrill buzzsaw voices, ignoring him. He walked through fields of sharp black rocks, stirring up swarms of buzzing flies with every step. The ammunition case was so heavy, and he was so little, it wasn't fair! It was surprising how few people there were on Mars. He supposed they must all be locked up underground or somewhere. Why couldn't he carry the gun instead? But he was. He was all alone with the gun, in that burnt-over landscape. The ashes got into his eyes so that he almost had to cry.

He walked toward the flame that burned at the horizon, holding the rifle on the ready. The man was shooting fire from a plastic garden hose, burning the rice; so he planted the butt of the rifle into the ground, because he was too little to shoot it any other way. He looked at the man with the garden hose, in his strange uniform. No man had ever seemed more hateful to Hansard than this one. The man Hansard turned the flame thrower on the boy Hansard, and they woke, both of them, screaming a single scream.

"It wasn't right," he said, astonished that it had taken himself so long to learn what, as soon as it had been spoken, seemed so self-evident.

And then, from another and not quite familiar part of his mind (as though, waking, he continued to dream), "It *isn't* right."

He shook his head sadly. Right or wrong, there was nothing *he* could do about it.

"But there *is*," the dream-voice insisted. The voice was his own and not his own. He relaxed and let himself smile. It was such a relief to have gone mad. It would be interesting to see what he did now. "Listen . . ." said the voice—his own and not his own—and he listened. . . .

SEVENTEEN

THE CATACLYSM

"Good-morning, Nathan! You seem to have recovered your appetite."

"Yes, and then some. No matter how much I seem to eat this morning, my stomach still feels hollow as a drum. Can you beat that?"

"And your good humor too. Welcome back to civilization. We've missed you."

"Just in the nick of time, eh?"

Pittmann regarded his subordinate uncertainly. Had this been said in jest? He decided it had been, but limited his show of appreciation to the barest smile.

131

"And you already have the coffee perking."

"I'm afraid I made it a little strong."

General Pittmann poured himself a cupful from the electric percolator and sipped the hot coffee appraisingly. "Yes, just a bit." It was a choice between making do with this, and waiting for another pot. He made do.

"I've been thinking . . ." Hansard said.

"We try to discourage thinking in the Army," Pittmann said placidly, as he pried apart two slices of frozen bread and put them into the toaster.

". . . about what you said the day I arrived here. I think you were right."

"I wouldn't be surprised." He grimaced over a second mouthful of the coffee. "But you'll have to refresh my memory, Nathan. I say so many right things."

"That it's genocidal to use the bombs."

"Did I say that? Surely only in the most hypothetical way—if I did. For my own part, I have little but contempt for people who warm their consciences over such words, and over that word especially. You can't win a war, you know, without making omelettes." Pleased with his timing, Pittmann cracked two eggs neatly into the electric skillet. "So I hope you're not taking such talk *too* seriously. At your age it isn't becoming to be that deadly earnest."

"But if the word has any meaning at all—"

"Exactly, Nathan. It has none. It's a red flag to wave at Liberals."

"There is the classic example."

"Yes?" General Pittmann looked up, inviting—or daring—Hansard to continue. An impish grin played at the corner of his lips. "The example of Germany, you mean? Why do you bring up a subject if you then refuse to talk about it? Auschwitz was ill-advised, certainly. A terrible waste of manpower, not to mention the prejudice involved; that is what *I* find most offensive. But nowadays prejudice doesn't enter into it. The bomb is the most democratic weapon man has ever devised. It draws absolutely no distinctions. . . . You make lousy coffee, Nathan."

"You make filthy jokes, General."

132

"That borders on impertinence, you know. But I'll over-look it for the sake of having you making conversation again."

"Your coffee will taste better if you put milk and sugar in it."

"A barbaric custom," Pittmann complained, but he fol-lowed Hansard's advice.

"Since when have you let considerations like that stand in your way?"

Pittmann laughed in good earnest. "Better, much better. You see, it's all in having a delicate touch. Would you like a piece of toast? Isn't life . . ." he scarcely seemed to pay attention to the knife that slipped out of his fingers and clattered on the floor, ". . . a terrible waste of manpower?" He laughed weakly.

"Oh, put that gun away, Nathan! What do you think I'm going to do—attack you with a butter knife? I'm too weak to . . . " he closed his eyes ". . . to finish sentences. It won't do you any good, Nathan, this noble gesture of yours. If you'd waited till the last minute, per-haps you might have prevented me. But then, this is only *one* post. What of the other? What of Russia? Foolish Nathan. . . .

"Why did you poison me?"

Hansard stared at the general coldly. Pittmann had very delicately balanced himself in the spindly tubular chair so that he could not fall out of it when he was un-conscious.

"I always wondered, you know . . . I always wondered what it would be like to die. I like it." He fell asleep, smiling.

Hansard chuckled. He knew Pittmann would be morti-fied when he woke up next day. There had been nothing but Army-issue barbiturates in the coffee, which were guaranteed nonlethal in any quantity. Hansard left the officers' mess, locking the door behind him.

He returned to his cabin to work on what Panofsky had promised would be "a trifle of rewiring." The adjustments that had to be made in the standard transmitter elements

133

that Hansard had rifled from storage taxed his manual abilities to the limit, but he had had the advantage of having performed the same task only hours before under Panofsky's supervision. It was exasperating just now, at the moment of highest crisis, to have to work electronic jigsaw puzzles. But it was possible. He needn't even feel rushed. Indeed, with so much at stake, he did not dare to.

When all the assemblies were put together and had been checked and rechecked, Hansard fitted them into two overnight bags—all but the essential "fix." This he hid in the observatory ventilation shaft.

As fate would have it, it was Worsaw whom he found on duty before the entrance to the manmitter.

"Private Worsaw, the General asked me to tell you to report to him on the double in the observatory."

"Sir?" Worsaw looked doubtful. It was not likely Pittmann would be interested in seeing *him*.

"I shall stand duty for you here, of course. Better not keep him waiting. I suspect his request has something to do with those chevrons missing from your sleeves." Hansard winked, a friendly conspirator's wink.

Worsaw saluted briskly and took his leave. *Poor fool,* Hansard thought. *He too walks out of my life smiling.* He was happy that he had not been required once again, and this time definitively, to kill Worsaw. He never wanted to kill anyone again.

Hansard entered the manmitter with the key he had taken from Pittmann. After taking out the first of the devices he would need, he depressed the button that operated the manmitter. The letters stencilled on the steel wall flickered from MARS to EARTH. He was home again, but there was no time to kiss the terran ground. His arrival would not have been unannounced; neither would it be welcome.

He looked at his watch. Two-eighteen P.M. He had, he estimated, another three minutes. He had found that he could hold his breath no longer than that. He made the last connections in the receiverless transmitter just as the door of the receiver sprang open and the guards burst in.

They opened fire on the man who was no longer there.

"Receiverless transmitters?" Hansard had objected, when first Panofsky had outlined his plan. "But you've said yourself that such a thing isn't possible. And it doesn't make *sense*."

"Sense!" Panofsky jeered. "What is sense? Does gravity make sense? Do wavicles? Does the Blessed Trinity? God glories in paradoxes more than in syllogisms. But I was quite sincere in what I told you. Strictly speaking, a receiverless transmitter isn't possible. But who says the receiver has to be where you want your bundles transmitted? Why not send it along *with* them?"

"Yes, and why don't I lift myself up by my boot straps?" Hansard replied sourly.

"The heart of the matter," Panofsky continued imperturbably, "lies in that word 'instantaneous.' If matter transmission is truly instantaneous and not just very very fast, like light, then, at the exact instant of transmission, where is the object we're transmitting? It is *here*, or is it *there*? And the answer, of course, is that it is both *here* and *there*. And thus—the receiverless transmitter, so-called. We just attach a set of three transmitters and three receivers to the object, posit the transmitters as being *here* and the receivers as being *there*, press the button, and *poof!* You see?"

Hansard shook his head glumly.

"But you've already *seen* it work! You traveled all over the house in it."

"Oh, I know it happened. But the state I'm in now, you could as easily convince me that it's magic that makes it work, as the laws of nature. That's what it is—even down to the magic number three."

"Numbers *are* magic, of course, and none more so than three. But there is also a reason for that number. Three points establish a plane. It is the hypothetical plane that those three receivers define by which we can place the transmitted object at exactly that point in space where we wish it to be."

"Even I can call your bluff on that one, Doctor. It takes four points to define an object's position in space. Three

135

will determine a plane, but for a solid body you need four. That's simple Euclidean geometry."

"And you'll get a good grade in that subject. In fact there does have to be a fourth transmitter-receiver for the whole thing to work at all. And the fourth one doesn't travel along with the others. It stays behind and serves as the point of reference. The 'here' posit of the transmitter and the 'there' posit of the receiver can be considered to form two immense pyramids sharing a common apex at the 'fix' point."

"And where will my fix be?"

"On Mars, of course. Where else could it be?"

Naturally enough, the first point for which Panofsky had been able to obtain exact information concerning longitude, latitude, and altitude had been his own residence, and it was there, in the library, that Hansard came first after leaving Camp Jackson/Virginia. Panofsky and Bridgetta being away in Moscow, Hansard was conveniently alone. He placed the first transmitter-receiver at the agreed-upon location behind the uniform edition of Bulwer-Lytton. Then, taking up the two bags with the rest of the equipment he set off once again, a comfortable thirty seconds ahead of schedule.

It had been more difficult to find sufficiently detailed information concerning two other locations. The data on the Great Pyramid of Egypt Panofsky had discovered in a back number of *The Journal of Theosophical Science*.

Hansard arrived at the apex of the Great Pyramid at night. He had never seen a desert from such a height under moonlight before and, despite the urgency of his task, he had to pause to gaze down at the scene with awe. Someone, perhaps a tourist, glimpsed Hansard's silhouette against the moon and began shouting at him. The night wind carried his words off and Hansard caught only scattered wisps of sound, not enough even to tell what language the man was speaking—much less his meaning. Hansard left the second of the transmitter-receivers atop the crumbling stone, and moved on to the third and last point of the triangulation.

He found himself in the midst of a vast concrete ex-

anse from which there projected, at wide intervals, the
mall knobs of the headstones. This was the eighty acres
f the Viet Nam War-Dead Memorial erected outside Can-
erra by the new Liberal Government that had taken Aus-
ralia out of the war. With a magnanimity unparalleled in
iistory, the government had here commemorated the
nemy's dead in equal number with its own.

Hansard set the last receiver-transmitter upon one of
he headstones. Only one minute twenty-three seconds had
assed since he'd made the first jump from Camp Jackson/
Virginia. There was time, some few seconds, for reverence.

"It was wrong," Hansard said with great definiteness.

And, though he did not go on to say so, the wrong was
rretrievable. The boy was dead forever. This very head-
tone might mark his grave.

That was all the time he could allow for reverence. He
ressed down the button of the third transmitter-receiver.
A delayed-action mechanism provided him with fifteen
econds' grace. He unzipped the second of the two bags
nd took out the neutralizer. It had an effective range of
ix feet.

"You'd better go now," he said to himself. It was Han-
ard$_2$ who said this, but there was no reply from Hansard$_1$.

Only then did Hansard$_2$ realize that he had been deceived
ll this while; that in an inviolable part of his mind, Han-
ard$_1$ had formed his intention and kept it secret from his
ther self. It was too late to argue with him, for suddenly
ie ground under Hansard$_2$'s feet became solid, and he
new that the earth had just been turned upside down on
s axis and transmitted to the other side of the solar
ystem.

"Impossible!" Hansard had said. "And if it *could* be
one, it would be a madness worse than the bombs."

"Fudge, Nathan! Haven't you learned yet that I'm al-
ays right?"

"What will become of all the people in the Real World?
ou should think of their welfare before you consider
urs."

"The chief immediate consequence for them will be
at people in the northern hemisphere will suddenly see

137

the constellations usual to southern skies. In consequence, there will probably be more than a few shipwrecks on the night-side of earth. A small enough price to pay, considering the alternative."

"But how will this prevent the bombs? They'll be coming from Mars to their receiver-satellites, in any case."

"But the receiver satellites will lie outside the earth's field of transmission. Earth-Sub-One will cross the solar system and leave the satellites behind."

"So they can drop their bombs on Earth-Sub-Two?"

"You forget that for anything constituted of primary matter, secondary matter seems not to exist. From the point of view of those bombs, earth will seem to have disappeared. Moreover, they will cease to be satellites, since the echo of earth remaining behind has no gravitational grip on them. They'll fly off tangent to their orbits and eventually be dragged down into the sun." Panofsky grinned. "Imagine, though, what your people on Mars will think when the earth suddenly disappears from the sky! Will they blame it on the Russians?"

Hansard was not ready to make jokes on the subject. "But . . . the magnitude of it! *The whole damn earth!*"

"Is that meant to be an objection? Great magnitudes often simplify an operation. Clock towers were built before wrist watches, and the solar system has often been called a celestial timepiece. Consider that, in transmitting the earth, I waste none of its momentum. Placed properly and pointed in the right direction, it should proceed in its immemorial orbit about the sun without a hairbreath of wobble. I can't guarantee quite *that* exactitude, but my calculations show that nothing too terrible should result."

"And turning it upside down?"

"To conserve the order of the seasons which, as you certainly should know, are caused by the earth's position along its orbit about the sun. In effect, I am advancing the earth six months through time. Turning it topsy-turvy will compensate for that exactly."

There was no air for him to breathe.

You fool! Hansard$_2$ thought angrily. *Why did you stay inside the field of neutralization? Why?*

What difference, now? There was a sadness in the tone of the reply that Hansard$_2$ could not believe to be his own. The six weeks they had lived apart had, after all, made them different men.

Do you suppose you're even now? Do you think your lost life can make up for his? Fool!

Not for his sake, no.

Then why? why? What of Bridgetta?

Hansard$_1$ did not, or could not, reply. Perhaps, for him, there would not have been a Bridgetta. Reluctantly Hansard$_2$ disengaged his body from its sheath of fibers. The discarded and soon lifeless body did not sink to the ground (which was not ground for it) but slowly, ever so slowly, lifted into the air and drifted above the vast concrete field, like a helium balloon, withered, at the end of a long day. The gravitational pull of the newly-created earth$_2$ had no effect upon the primary matter of that body, and it was being pulled inexorably toward the Real Moon low in the West, hidden behind clouds.

The moon, in turn, had begun its slow plunge toward the sun. There was no longer any force to hold it in place.

A residue at the back of Hansard$_2$'s mind told him why his sub-one self had gone willingly to his own death. He was ashamed of having, to his way of thinking, been guilty of that most heinous of crimes—mutiny.

Hansard$_2$ removed the breathing equipment he had been wearing since the night before. He did not need it, for now he had a world of air to breathe again, a world of ground to walk upon, and a world of men to give meaning to his own manhood. This, the echo of a world, was *his* Real World now.

And there would not be a war to destroy it.

EIGHTEEN

THE HAPPY ENDING

Hansard's taxi came to a stop outside the New St. George, a hotel which in the ordinary scheme of things he would not have been able to afford. He asked the man at the desk the number of Panofsky's suite. It was, perhaps, not wholly by chance, the same that Hansard had occupied, invisibly, forty days before. He found the two Panofskys alone.

"Nathan! How good to see you, Nathan!" They drove their wheel chairs toward him with one accord, braking just short of a collision.

"I was afraid," said the Panofsky in the skullcap, "that I would have to leave without seeing you."

"He's off to Rome, you know," the other Panofsky explained, "to see the Pope. For the time being, anyone who travels via transmitter is under Vatican interdict; so Bernard will fly. You flew yourself, didn't you, Nathan?" Hansard nodded. "But it took you such a long time!"

"The Egyptian emigration authorities were just a little upset to find me in their country. And then, when the moon began to disappear . . ."

"Ooof, the moon! I am so stupid, I deserve not to live. A kick in the pants I deserve."

Hansard was skeptical. "You can't mean that you actually *overlooked* that this would happen? That you thought of everything but that?"

The two Panofskys exchanged a guilty look. "Such at least," the first said mildly, "we have given the government to believe."

"But let's not speak of it, for though the government is treating us a little more civilly now, this room is surely bugged. Tell me, Nathan, do you think the end justifies the means? Once in a while, perhaps? It is true that without the moon there will be no tides, either here or on Earth-Sub-One; the ocean currents will become confused, and there will be terrible disasters, yes—disorders, tragedies. But on the other hand there has not been a war. Besides, I have a plan in readiness—it is being explained now to the Russians—for recovering the moon. But you had better explain it to Nathan, Bernard; I'm late for my plane. Is there anything I can do for you in Rome, Nathan? Arrange a wedding, perhaps, at St. John Lateran?"

"Off to His Holiness, busybody! You know the Captain dislikes to be nudged.

"The moon," he continued, when his double had departed, "is at this moment populated by a number of very perplexed, not to say frantic scientists—Russians—none of whom have an inkling of what is happening to the solar system. Similarly, on Earth-Sub-One, no one will have any notion of what's going on—no one but myself, Panofsky-Sub-One, and even he may be upset to think that someone else has, all unknown to him, developed a receiverless transmitter and put it to such apocalyptic use.

"Here, meanwhile, I have been explaining—to the President, to committees of every kind, finally even to the press—what has been done and why. And though they are all very outraged, I think they are secretly glad—like a matador waking up in a hospital, amazed at still being alive after his excesses of courage. They have listened to me, and a few have understood. Those who didn't understand believed.

"So, this is what is being done: A number of our military and scientific personnel have been transmitted to Earth-Sub-One, and there they will try to do what you did—reintegrate with their sub-one selves. When any one of them has accomplished this, he will use a receiverless transmitter to travel to the moon, dealing with that body as you have dealt with the earth.

"The moon-sub-one will be returned to its proper orbit, leaving behind a sub-two echo which can then be returned to *its* proper orbit, leaving behind a sub-three moon, sad to say, will have to fall into the sun . . . unless its sub-

141

three inhabitants, still equipped with receiverless transmitters, decide to take it somewhere else. And why shouldn't they? While their stores last they can travel anywhere in the universe. Perhaps that moon will be the first interstellar voyager.

"It is all very complicated, isn't it? If you'd like to take a bath, our suite has three *huge* bathtubs. I always find that a bath helps when things become too complicated."

"Thank you, not a bath. But I had hoped . . . ?"

"Of course, Nathan! Of course she is here. Enter! Enter, Bridgetta!"

She rode in on ripples of laughter. He did not know which Bridgetta she was, Bridie, Jet, Bridget, or any other. But it made no difference. They were all but a single woman whom he loved, and he embraced her, saying, "Darling," and they kissed, a kiss that was like laughing still.

"Professor Panofsky," said Hansard stiffly (though there was now a kind of grace in his stiffness that had not been there before), "I would like to ask for the hand of your wife Bridgetta in marriage."

"You have my blessings, both of you, but first you had better come to an understanding with your rivals."

"No," Hansard said, "this time it is for *her* to decide how she wants to dispose of *me*."

"Not Bridgetta's rivals, Nathan, *yours*." And with a flourish of laughter, of music, the two Nathan Hansards who had been waiting in the adjoining room entered, arm-in-arm with two more Bridgettas. They arranged themselves before him with the modest symmetry of a Mozart finale. He had known they would be here, he had known it these many days (since, after all, he was not the final, the Australian Hansard$_2$, but the penultimate Hansard$_2$ who had remained behind after the transmission to Canberra, an echo atop the Great Pyramid), and yet he had not till now believed it. He grasped each of their extended hands in his own, and they stood there so a little while, as though about to begin a children's ring-game.

And here *we* are, quite at the end of our story—or very

close to the end. Our hero is to be rewarded for his labors; the world is saved from annihilation; even the moon has been recovered, and Panofsky, for the first time in his life, is free. Now is the loveliest of June weather, though (it is true) one has to go outside the dome to appreciate the young summer in all its glory. Now is the perfect time to take a boat out on the river, or just go walking along country roads, though these (it is true) become harder and harder to find.

But perhaps for our hero it will not be hard at all. Love bathes all landscapes in a softening light. It is only ourselves, at our greater distance, with our cooler view, who may feel a little sad to think that the world's loveliness will not always and everywhere bear too close examination.

However, even that is changing! Even the world will change now and become a better world, milder and mightier, and more humane. There will be power, and power to spare, to do all the things that were so hard to do till now. There will be no more boundaries, but everywhere freedom and unconstraint. There will be no more war. There will be room to move about in, places to go, destinies—all the universe, in fact. What a splendid world! What grand fun it would be to live there!

But it is too late, for we are now quite at the end of *our* story. The rest belongs to them.

It had been a wedding in the grand manner—cascades of white lace, orange blossoms, organ music, a minister with the broadest, the stateliest, of *A*'s. And now they stood—Hansard and Bridgetta, and Hansard and Bridgetta, and Hansard and Bridgetta—on the threshold of the transmitter. Each couple had chosen a different destination for their honeymoon; the first to Ceylon, the second a cruise up the Amazon, and the third . . .

"Are you ready?" Panofsky asked.

In reply Hansard lifted up his bride and carried her over the threshold. Panofsky pushed the button that would transmit them to the Vatican. Hansard had never before seen the Sistine Chapel. He gasped.

Hansard sighed. "It doesn't seem to be working, does it?"

Bridgetta laughed softly, without stopping to nibble at his ear.

He carried her back across the threshold, through the closed door. Hansard and Bridgetta, and Hansard and Bridgetta, were waiting for them outside the transmitter. They pointed to Panofsky, who was writing on a note pad on the worktable. Panofsky finished the note, turned and smiled, though it could not be said he smiled quite at them, and left the room.

Unthinkingly, Hansard tried to pick the piece of paper off the table. The tertiary flesh of his hand passed through the secondary matter.

It was now as it had been: The pumps that had been pumping air to Mars were pumping still, though they pumped air of second-degree reality, which left behind the echo of an echo, and this air the six lovers, themselves the echoes of their echoes, could breathe.

"What does it say?" asked Bridgetta, though she could read the note as well as Hansard. But she wanted to hear him say the words:

"Happy Honeymoon."